Trapper Boy

by Hugh R. MacDonald

Cape Breton University Press
Sydney, Nova Scotia, Canada

To my wife, Joanne,
and to the memory of our beloved son, Keith.

Cape Breton University Press recognizes the support of the Canada Council for the Arts, Block Grant program, and the Province of Nova Scotia, through the Department of Communities, Culture and Heritage, for our publishing program. We are pleased to work in partnership with these bodies to develop and promote our cultural resources.

Cover art: Patsy MacAulay MacKinnon © 2012
Cover layout: Gail Jones, Sydney, NS
Author photo: Michael G. MacDonald
Mining sketches: Michael G. MacDonald
Layout: Mike Hunter, Port Hawkesbury and Sydney, NS
First printed in Canada
Second printing 2013

Library and Archives Canada Cataloguing in Publication
MacDonald, Hugh R., 1956-
Trapper boy : a novel / Hugh R. MacDonald.

ISBN 978-1-897009-73-4
Web PDF 978-1-927492-10-9
EPUB 978-1-897009-93-2
Mobi 978-1-897009-94-9
I. Title.

PS8625.D637T73 2012   C813'.6   C2012-903186-0

Cape Breton University Press
P.O. Box 5300
Sydney, Nova Scotia B1P 6L2 Canada

www.cbupress.ca

RECYCLED
Paper made from recycled material
FSC® C103567

Trapper Boy

by Hugh R. MacDonald

Illustrations by Michael G. MacDonald

Cape Breton University Press
Sydney, Nova Scotia, Canada

Chapter 1

John Wallace Donaldson awoke, looked at the calendar and jumped from his bed. It was June 28, 1926. It was grading day, and JW was in the running for some of the prizes.

Mostly everyone called him JW. He was proud that he was named for his two grandfathers, John on his mother's side and Wallace on his father's, but only his mother and some other grown-ups called him by his full name.

JW had studied hard and knew he was close to the top of the class in both English and French. There were cash awards, but if he won any of those, he had already promised the money to his mother – the silver dollar would go a long way toward necessities. The English prize was the one he coveted: a set of books, consisting of some of the classics. He had already borrowed some of them from the small town library, but to own the books and to be able to read them whenever he wanted was something beyond belief.

His father had told him many times to get his nose out of the books, but JW knew his father was secretly proud that he was doing so well in school. His mother had told him.

The water in the bucket was cool. JW poured some into the small wash basin and splashed it on his face, chasing away the night's cobwebs. He hadn't slept well, his mind racing with the hope of winning the books. Pirates and knights and thoughts of far-off places had kept him awake, following him to his dreams where he had saved a beautiful princess and fought pirates for their gold.

The kitchen stove was crackling from the kindling used to start the fire. Before long, coal would be added to create a base. It was the end of June, and the stove no longer had to be banked overnight. A new fire was started each morning, unless a few embers remained from the previous night that could be coaxed back to life. JW listened to his mother lifting the lid on the stove, adding coal from the scuttle.

"John Wallace," his mother called. "Run out and get a few eggs for your father, dear. I expect him along any minute. Try to squeeze a few drops from the goat, if you want some milk for the porridge." Eggs were saved for his father's meal, but JW didn't really like eggs that much anyway. The porridge suited him fine.

"Alright, Ma," he said, picking up the milking dish from the table. The goat didn't always want to part with her milk, but he usually managed to get enough to cover their needs. He spotted his father a quarter of a mile down the road and raised his arm to wave, then watched as his father's arm rose to return the greeting.

The small group of chickens moved aside as JW reached under the first one. An indignant squawk pierced the morning quiet. Rummaging through several nests, he picked up the morning bounty, four eggs, and took them to his mother.

"Da's on his way," he said, placing the eggs in the centre of the table, ensuring they couldn't roll off and splatter on the floor. He hurried outside to get the milk.

JW wanted to be at the table when his father sat down. Pirates and knights from the books were exciting, but it was his father who had instilled a love of stories in him as a small child. JW had turned thirteen a month earlier. He still loved to listen as his father recounted his work in the coal mine, telling of finding fossils of long-dead animals and plant life, and of cave-ins that caused the men to seek cover from falling debris. He loved the stories, but had no intention of ever working in the mines.

"How'd it go in the pit last night, Da?" JW asked, his spoon coming automatically to his mouth as he stared at his father. Some days, JW saw the wrinkles in his father's face, and today he noticed the creases seemed deep. He never wanted to believe his dad was getting old or tired, but today he didn't talk much, as if the effort would tax the last of his strength. JW knew something was bothering his father, but he also knew it wasn't his place to ask what it was. His father would tell him in due time.

"I'll tell you what. How 'bout I tell you tomorrow? I'm all talked out, and it's all I can do to have a cuppa tea," his father said.

"Sure, Da. I gotta get to school anyway. Today's the last day and I want to get there early," JW said, his mind once again filled with the prospect of winning the books. "Thanks for the porridge, Ma," he said, as he rose from the table. He rushed upstairs, hearing his father speak in a low voice to his mother.

The satchel that he used to carry his books had been a gift from his grandfather, as was the house they lived in. He pulled the satchel from the top of his bookshelf and filled it with the books that had to be returned now that the end of the school year had arrived. His teacher, Mrs. Johnson, had agreed to give him some books that were not suitable for distribution the following year. Some of the kids took better care of the books than others did, and there were books that just wore out from use. JW had a complete set of his school books from primary to grade seven, and he hoped he'd be able to get a set of this year's grade-eight books as well. He had every one of his scribblers piled neatly on the shelves, from the primary primers to his notes from this year.

JW could barely remember his grandfather, who had died when JW was five, but he remembered the day his grandfather gave him the satchel.

"This you can use for your books, lad. It's made out of fine leather and should last a lifetime. There's lots of pockets in it too, where you can hide your secrets. I made it special for you. Something you can remember me by. You're a fine lad," his grandfather had said, as he'd rubbed JW's head and patted his back.

JW hadn't known his grandfather had been ill and near death when he'd presented him with the satchel. He only knew that he and his parents had gone to live with him after Grandma Donaldson had gone to heaven.

Grandpa Donaldson had been a blacksmith, shoeing horses and making leather products as well as tools for the miners, including the shovel and pick that JW's father used. Several saddles and bridles remained in the barn. They were old and the leather was cracked in places, but his father left them hanging on the rafters, spiders encasing them in silky webs. Their horse, Lightning, had never been broken to a saddle and was instead used for plowing a patch of earth to plant vegetables each year and hauling wood for winter. He was accustomed to a harness and bridle only.

JW took the stairs two at a time for he knew it was getting late. The clock chimed, signalling it was eight o'clock. He'd have to hurry now to be early for class. School was something he loved, though he thoroughly enjoyed the summers off as well. Sure, he had to tend the garden, but he had lots of time to fish and lie under a tree and read books about England and Scotland and France, as well as Africa and Arabia. Not having to write book reports about them was also nice. He shouted a goodbye to his parents as he rushed out the front door. It was strange to still see them sitting at the table, their heads bowed low, almost as if in prayer, their voices hushed. Adults had a lot to worry about; he was in no hurry to become one.

He put the long leather strap of the satchel over his shoulder and started off at a slow jog, the satchel tapping lightly against his side, matching the rhythm of his pace. He slowed as he drew near to his friend Beth Jessome's house. Beth was also in the running for the English prize. JW really liked her, but he hoped he'd win. He knew that if she won she would lend him the books, but it wouldn't be the same as owning them. He had already cleared a place for them on his bookshelf.

He saw her looking out the window, waiting for him. He flushed a little as he recalled some of the kids at school saying they were boyfriend and girlfriend. Sure, he liked her, but they weren't dating. Last year they had kissed, but only once. He wondered if that *did* mean they might be boyfriend and girlfriend. He pushed the thought aside as she came out to meet him.

"Are you excited that it's grading day?" Beth asked.

"I sure am. Who do you think's gonna win the English prize?"

"I don't know, but it might be one of us," Beth answered. "Still, it could be three or four others. I hope it's me or you."

"Yeah," JW said, his mind not wanting to comprehend that perhaps someone else could win and he'd never get to read the books. "Yeah, me or you."

"What are you going to do with all your time off?" Beth asked.

"Remember the old fort Mickey and I built in grade six?"

"Yes," Beth said, nodding her head.

"Well, I plan to fix it up and sleep in it some nights. It's right up by the swimming hole, not far from where I like to fish. Ma doesn't mind, as long as I get my chores done first."

Beth told him of the things she had planned for the summer, and they agreed that maybe they would meet at the fort for some swimming and picnics.

"How is Mickey doing?" Beth asked.

"I don't know," he answered. "He doesn't come around much anymore. The last time I went to his house, his mother told me he was sleeping and that he doesn't have time to play. She didn't tell me not to come back, but that's the impression I got. She said he needs his sleep. I guess his work at the mines is tough. I haven't been back to his house since, but I miss him."

"I heard he's no longer working on the surface, that he's gone down into the mine," Beth said.

JW stopped walking and stared at her. "When did this happen?" he asked.

"About a month ago. His mother told Ma that he's getting along well but that he finds the time long. He's working as a trapper boy," Beth said.

"He can't like that too much. He doesn't like the dark." JW didn't bother adding that he found the dark unnerving also. His own plans of sleeping in the fort would only be on moonlit nights, and then only if his dog, Gulliver, would stay the night.

JW knew there were different jobs in the mine. He knew that a trapper boy opened and closed a trap door, but he had no idea what the conditions were like. He planned to become an explorer, or a captain of a ship, and travel to exotic places. But first he was looking forward to college. Mrs. Johnson had explained to him that with an education he could do anything he wanted.

Chapter 2

"Everyone take their seat," Mrs. Johnson said. "After today, many of you will be going on to high school. I will miss you, but I'll see you from time to time. If you ever have any questions, please feel free to come and see me." She cleared her throat and said, "It's time to award the prizes to the top students in French and English. The French award goes to John Wallace Donaldson. *Très bon, Jean,*" Mrs. Johnson said.

"*Merci beaucoup, Madame,*" JW said, accepting the silver dollar, sliding it into one of the pockets of his satchel. He anxiously waited to hear her announce the winner of the English prize.

"Although there was only one prize in the French category, I'm happy to say there are a few prizes in the English one. It was a very tight race, and I'm proud of all of you. As you know, the first place winner will receive a set of five books."

JW looked around the classroom, trying to figure out who the other winners might be.

"Third prize goes to William Gillis. Well done, Billy."

JW watched as Billy put the coin in his pocket and returned to his seat. *One down,* he thought.

"Second prize goes to …"

All eyes turned to the classroom door as Mr. Robinson, the principal, entered the room.

"Good morning, children."

"Good morning, sir," they replied.

"Congratulations to all of you heading to high school next year. Enjoy your summer."

"Thank you, sir."

Mr. Robinson nodded at Mrs. Johnson and left the room.

"Where were we? Oh yes. Second prize goes to Daniel Harrietha. Well done, Danny."

JW saw that Danny received money, as well as a ribbon for second place. He shifted about nervously in his seat as he waited for the first place winner to be announced. He'd been sure that either he or Beth would win, but there was only one prize remaining, and that meant one of them would go home empty-handed.

"And now, first place goes to Beth Jessome," Mrs. Johnson said. "Congratulations, Beth."

JW's heart sank as he watched Beth walk to the front of the class to accept her prize. He'd noticed she'd looked at him on her way. His eyes were drawn to the set of books she carried back to her desk. He couldn't believe that he hadn't even placed in the top three. He had worked so hard.

"And the other first prize winner is John Wallace Donaldson. Congratulations, John Wallace. The first time we've ever had a tie."

JW looked at Mrs. Johnson, who was smiling, then looked at Beth. It took him a moment to understand that he'd won too, and he started smiling. He looked at his teacher's desk, but didn't see any more books. His elation was short lived. He supposed his mother would be happy with another silver dollar, but he'd had his heart set on winning the books.

He rose from his desk and started toward the front of the class, when Beth pulled at his shirt.

"Sit down! Mrs. Johnson said she will see you after class," Beth said, trying to keep her voice low. But one kid snickered, "Look at the love birds."

JW dropped back into his seat, his shoulders slumped. He had worked so hard for the books, but at least Beth had them. He wondered if she'd trade him for the silver dollar. Instantly he knew he couldn't even ask her, because he had already promised his mother the silver dollar. Mrs. Johnson called everyone's name as she handed out the report cards. JW saw several kids hang their heads when they learned they would have to repeat the grade again. His mood changed when he considered how fortunate he was to be going to high school next year.

All his classmates had left before Mrs. Johnson called him to the front of the class. He shuffled forward, trying to put a smile on his face.

"I have those grade-eight books that you asked for. Some of them are not in the greatest of shape, but all the pages are intact. Why is it that you want them?" Mrs. Johnson asked.

"I love books, and in case I ever want to check on something, I'll know right where to look." JW hesitated for a moment before adding, "I was helping Mickey Mc-Guire for awhile after he went to the coal mines, but the hours were too long for him in the pit, so he had to give it up. If he ever wants to pick it up again, I got all the books and scribblers. I mean I *have* all the books and scribblers." JW smiled again. "Thanks for all the help this year, Mrs. Johnson."

"You're welcome. It was a pleasure having you in the class," she said, handing him a small box. "I put your prize in with the school books. Have a great summer."

"You too, ma'am," JW said. He hurried to catch up with Beth.

"What did she want to see you after class for?" Beth asked.

"She had some old school books that I asked her for," JW said, holding up the small box. His eyes wandered to her prize. He could see *Treasure Island* and *The Count of Monte Cristo* on the top. He didn't need to ask to see the others, because he knew every title that was in the set of five books. He wondered if Beth cherished the books the same way he did. He put his satchel over one shoulder and moved the box to one arm. "Want me to carry your books?" he asked.

"I think you got just about all you can handle," Beth said. "But thanks just the same."

They talked about winning the English prize and promised to meet tomorrow to discuss fixing up the old fort, both agreeing that it would make a great place to change into their swimming clothes. The walk home from school always seemed longer because there was no hurry to get home. Beth's mother was waiting in the doorway as they arrived at her house.

"Are you coming in then, John Wallace?" Beth's mother asked.

"No, ma'am. Ma's waiting," JW answered. Saying goodbye to Beth and Mrs. Jessome, he headed for home.

Chapter 3

JW pushed open the door leading to the kitchen. His mother was busy putting biscuits in to bake, and he could smell the stew that was bubbling on the back of the stove. Large beads of sweat glistened on his mother's forehead. The temperature had to be in the nineties. The coal stove's fire was raging, and with the temperature pushing seventy outside, he wondered how she could stand the heat.

She turned to face him. "Well then, how did you do?" she asked, taking his report card from his hand. "My, but you done grand," she said. "Did you win the books like you hoped?"

"No, I tied for first prize, but Beth got the books. I think I got another dollar," JW said and noticed the excited look in his mother's eyes.

"I'm sorry you didn't win the books, dear, but the dollar will come in handy," his mother said.

"Yeah, I know, Ma." He pulled the dollar from his satchel. "This one's for the French prize, and this one," he said, opening the box, "is for ..." JW's eyes opened wide. The five books that Beth received weren't the only set. He had his own set too. "Oh gee, Ma, look, I got books too," JW said, filled with the glee that only total surprise can bring about.

"Goodness, you won both the French and English prizes! My, but aren't you the smart one," his mother said. "Your father will be proud. You've got more schooling than half the county, all you'll ever need."

"No way, Ma! I plan on going to college, so I can visit faraway lands," he said. "I'll show Da later. Right now I gotta feed Lightning and pull a few weeds." JW went upstairs to change.

Chapter 4

Lightning gave a low whinny as JW entered the barn and moved aside as he shovelled out the stall. Then the horse stood patiently as JW lifted and cleaned each hoof, patted Lightning's withers, filled the bucket with water and threw fresh hay in the stall. Their old horse was named Lightning because of a jagged patch of white on his forehead that resembled a bolt of lightning and stood out against his black coat. Lightning wasn't really a pet, but JW treated him well. He earned his keep by plowing the patch of earth where they planted vegetables in the spring, and he put his head down in the fall as he pulled home the wood that would supplement the coal used during the winter months. Like all the other miners, his father had had his working hours cut, and JW knew that the days his father had off would be used to get wood. He had spent some time during the previous summer working in the woods with his father and expected to do the same this year.

Gulliver waited for JW to come out of the barn. His tail wagged and his head shook, while the rest of him went into a full-body shuffle. They were best friends. JW reached down with his left hand and ran his fingers through Gulliver's fur. He picked up the hoe with his right hand. "Wish the vegetables grew as fast as the weeds, ole boy," he said. He walked between the rows and noticed that the carrots and turnips were beginning to sprout, as well as the lettuce and radishes. The big patch of potatoes was on the other side of the barn and was a tomorrow job. He and his father had planted extra this year. JW remembered some of the miners coming to their house during the past winter and his father giving away some of the food they had stored. The men's faces were gaunt. The long strike of 1925 had taken its toll. The Company Store had closed as a result of the strike, and the out-of-work miners had nowhere to turn and no way to feed their families. They were proud men, reduced to asking for help from friends.

JW's stomach growled. The sun was heading toward the west, so he knew there were only a few hours of sunlight left in the day. He hurried to the kitchen. "Ma, can I get a bite of the stew so I can go fishing?" he asked. He watched her fill a bowl. "Where's Da?"

"He's been kinda restless today, so he's still lying down," his mother answered.

"He's alright though?" JW asked. He remembered how tired his father had looked this morning.

"Just tired is all, dear," she said. "When are you gonna start on the fort?" she asked, changing the subject.

"Tomorrow, after I get the potatoes weeded, so I have to get up early," he answered.

JW ate the stew quickly and thanked his mother, then grabbed his fishing pole. He stopped behind the barn, where he moved aside a few boards and picked a dozen fat worms out of the ground below. An old rusted can lay close by into which he put a little earth, then the worms. Gulliver bounded along beside him, happy to be with his master, as they ran the last five hundred feet to the muddy riverbank.

There had been a lot of rain this spring, and the water in the brook was deep and moved quickly. JW dropped a piece of deadwood into the stream and watched the currents pull it toward the pond that flowed through to St. Andrews Channel, then out to the ocean.

JW imagined himself as captain of the deadwood ship, travelling the raging waters, skilfully manoeuvring each twist and turn. He ran alongside on the bank, following his ship. He no longer cared about the fish in the brook. He was more interested in the ship's journey to distant lands.

The piece of deadwood entered the pond, currents hurrying it toward the mouth where the beaver dam usually kept the water level high. JW noticed the dam had broken away, and water flowed freely to the mouth and out to the waiting lake. He watched the deadwood ship go under the train trestle on its way to the lake, the ocean and to lands filled with mystery and adventure.

Gulliver barked and the spell was broken.

"Let's go, fella. Time to catch some fish." Retracing his steps, JW noticed a dark pool that appeared deep and still. The worm on his hook dangled as he dropped it into the deep water. Immediately, the line pulled tight and the rod bent almost in half. Thinking the line was snagged, JW pulled the rod sharply to one side hoping to loosen the hook. He was amazed to see the biggest trout he had ever seen jump from the water. His knees trembled and his hands shook. The trout disappeared under the water again, and JW thought it had escaped the hook. Then it surfaced again, and he felt like Captain Ahab trying to capture Moby Dick.

The fishing rod was an old one; his grandfather had owned it. He had heavy-gauge line tied to the top two eyelets. The piece of line was about twenty feet in length. His excitement grew as the tip of the rod continued to bend closer to the ground. He expected it to break at any moment. He was sure he would lose the fish, leaving only a "one that got away" story. His arms flexed as he tried to prevent the fish from escaping downstream. JW stood his ground and then decided to head upstream against the current. At first the strain seemed too much, but little by little, JW felt the trout weaken. He pulled old Moby from the water and watched as it gasped, its energy spent. He had won the battle, but didn't feel that great about it as he watched his opponent struggling for life, the hook lying beside it. Somehow the hook had only held long enough to land the mammoth fish.

The trout was longer than his forearm. Several scars, from other battles, marked its face. JW stood in amazement before bending to pick up Moby. It seemed to weigh a hundred pounds, but he knew it was closer to four or five, which was still huge by all accounts. His heart wasn't into eating this majestic fish.

"Whatcha got there?"

JW startled at the voice behind him. He turned to see his father.

"Wow, that's some fish," his father said. "I heard stories about trout this size, but that's the biggest I ever seen. We could stuff him if you'd like."

"You know what I'd really like to do? Set him free," JW said. As if on cue, the fish snapped its large tail and fell to the ground. Its next move sent it over the bank and into the water. It spent a moment on the surface, winded by the exertion, then snapped its tail and dove deep into the water.

They laughed and talked of the size of the fish and of the fine job JW had done in school as they headed toward home. They had caught enough fish to make the evening's meal, only briefly mentioning to JW's mother the big fish that got away. He wasn't sure she would have understood his desire to set it free.

Chapter 5

The goat had been unusually kind earlier that morning, standing still as JW filled the milk container. He splashed milk on the porridge his mother placed before him and added brown sugar. He held his spoon above his bowl, waiting until his father's breakfast was laid on the table. JW hoped his father was in a storytelling mood after the long night in the mine.

"How was your shift, Da?" he asked. "Anything exciting happen?" His eyes were filled with wonder. The world was a magical place to JW, and he loved to experience adventure, even vicariously. He waited as his father cleared his throat.

"Remember I told you about tunnel nine?"

"Yeah," his son said, nodding.

"The water's still trickling in, more like a small stream now. Arty McCleary saw something moving at his feet and near fainted. He took off running in a hurry. Left the pony standing there. Musta been a half hour before he came back. I thought it was only a rat, but when I got my lamp fixed on it…" JW's father paused, then wiped a hand across his face. "It had two big eyes and horns sticking out on its head. No arms or legs, but it had a long skinny body. On its face was a long white beard, and it spoke to me," his father said.

"What did it say?" JW asked, feeling the hair on his neck rise, even though it was daytime.

"It said 'Tell your boy thanks for letting my grandson go yesterday.'"

"What?" JW said, then burst out laughing, realizing his father had been pulling his leg. "Good one, Da. You sure had me going. I thought there were monsters in the mine."

"You shouldn't be filling his head with scary things down in the pit," his mother said.

"Oh, we were just having a little bit a fun, dear. He's not scared, are you, JW?"

"No, sir, but it doesn't matter, 'cause I'm never going down there anyhow. I'm gonna ride camels through the desert and sail the seven seas. Yes, sir, that's what I'm gonna do. You know they say the pyramids have been standing for thousands of years and no one knows how they were built? I wanna see them with my own eyes. Can't you just picture that, eh, Ma? When I become a ship's captain, I'll take you with me. You too, Da, if you wanna come."

JW noticed his parents had become quiet, but he didn't know why. His father's breakfast was only half eaten but was pushed to the middle of the table signalling that he was finished. The table was cleared, and it was obvious that the conversation was over for that morning.

"I'm going down to work on the fort and maybe do some fishing. Beth is going to meet me later. I'll see you in a few hours," he said, receiving only a muffled response. His parents stayed at the table talking. Taking a long-sleeved shirt to keep the mosquitoes and black flies off, JW left the house. He wondered what they were talking about but knew there were adult conversations and that it was not his place to ask. His curiosity faded when he spotted Beth on the path just ahead of him. He ran to catch up with her, all thoughts of his parents gone for the moment.

Chapter 6

"What were you thinking? Filling his head with creatures and such. You had *me* scared. In another month or two, the boy could be heading into the pit himself," Mary Donaldson said.

"That's just it. I wasn't thinking. How can we send him into that black hole? He's not ready for it. I don't think he ever will be," Andrew Donaldson said.

"You think I want him to go there? If the wages get rolled back again, we'll need two wages to make one," Mary said. Tears had sprung to her eyes, and she wiped them away. "God, I wish there was another way, but I can't see how."

Andrew rose from his chair and put his arms around her. "I'll start getting him ready tomorrow, but I wanna take it slow, so don't tell him yet. I'll show him what it's like down there." He kissed her forehead, then shuffled across the floor to the bedroom. Andrew doubted he would sleep, but hoped that some of the tension would leave his tired body when he stretched out on the bed.

Every time the coal company needed money they just took it off the men. At least that was how it seemed to Andrew. The new owners had rolled the wages back so often that he was making less than he had been five years earlier, but the cost of food and necessities continued to rise. He had planned on putting in a much larger garden this year, but he didn't have enough money to buy many more seeds. Still, the garden was a little bigger than last year's. His paycheque went to pay his bill at the Co-op store, and he was forced to charge more food and other needed items. Although the company-owned stores that had kept the men like indentured servants had closed, he still never seemed to have any money. He closed his eyes, sighing loudly, willing sleep to come.

Chapter 7

JW watched as his father's hand sketched the underground scene.

"This is what young Mickey is doing these days," his father said as he pushed the paper across the table. "The large door opens to allow the horse and cart through, but you have to be quick to shut the door, 'cause that's what keeps the air in the mine. It's an important job. You can't slack off when you're working the trap doors. A trapper boy can't sleep or daydream on the job. If the door's left open, men can suffocate. Everyone could die."

Looking at the large door in the picture, JW drew a breath. Poor Mickey. The horse and cart followed railway tracks, and he found himself wondering where they led and what lay beyond the trap door. He wanted to ask but knew the stories were done for the day when his father rose from the table.

"Can I keep the picture?" JW asked. "I'd like to put it up on my wall." The blackened face of the trapper boy actually looked like his friend Mickey.

JW hadn't known his father could draw so well. Pulling the picture closer, he saw the sad, tired look of his friend. The phrase "old before his time" came to mind, and now he understood its meaning.

"Sure, you can keep it. I'll draw you a new one tomorrow," his father said. Andrew Donaldson headed toward his bedroom. "Maybe we'll go fishing Sunday, JW," he called from the bedroom.

"That would be great, Da. Goodnight," JW said. Even though it was morning, it was nighttime for his father.

The picture of Mickey scared him. He could imagine several rats in the corner, waiting to get through the trap door. He shuddered at the thought of rats coming so close in the dark mine. He steered clear of the ones in the barn, and they ran whenever someone came near.

He had never really thought about the harshness that the boys and men in the mines had to endure until now. Long hours, little pay and a boss who rolled back your wages every time he suffered a loss. His parents hadn't told him much, but his room was above the kitchen, and the vent in the ceiling came directly into his room. Their voices were as clear as a foghorn on a foggy night. Often, they sounded as if they were right next to him. He tried not to listen, but sometimes curiosity got the best of him.

JW knew about the mine owners and the man, Roy Wolvin, who'd become known as Roy the Wolf because of his total disregard for the men and their families. His father had told him that as the president of BESCO – British Empire Steel Corporation – Wolvin controlled the lives and livelihood of both the steelworkers and the coal miners. But JW had dismissed this as another grown-up problem. He now understood that without enough money paid to the men, times were going to get tougher. Talks of strikes and the increase in the food and supply prices meant people were going to go hungry, especially if the strikes happened. If Roy the Wolf had his way, the rollbacks would have the same effect.

JW went to his room and neatly tacked the picture to his wall. Sitting on his bed, he stared at the picture for a long time. It was only noon, but he lay down, continuing to stare at the picture. A light rain was falling and he lis-

tened to the rhythmic sound it made against his window and felt himself drift off to sleep.

His dreams were vivid but not of pirates and pyramids. The rats had huge teeth and they carried off lunch boxes and hissed at him as he shooed them away. The trap door was heavy and he had to pull it open every five minutes. Men with blank faces passed by, never speaking with him, just shouting orders to the horses and to him.

JW startled awake. He sat up in his bed, surprised that he had fallen asleep at that hour of the day. Trembling at the memory of the dream, he looked at the picture on his wall.

The rain had stopped, so he decided it was a good time to weed the potato patch. The sooner it was done, the sooner he could get back to work on the old fort. There were only a couple of months of summer, and then he would be off to high school. He wanted to enjoy as much fishing and swimming as he could get. You only get to be a kid once, he concluded, and he knew that Mickey hadn't gotten the chance. He wished that his friend could be there with him but knew Mickey had to get his rest to carry out the mind-numbing job of sitting in the dark waiting for horses and rats.

Pulling on his old clothes, JW descended the stairs quietly, not wanting to wake his father. The memory of the picture haunted him as he thought of Mickey. Fear crept into his thoughts as he remembered the importance his father had put on the details of the trap door. He didn't want to think about the mines anymore and pushed the thought aside as he went outside. He finished the weeding in no time and sat with his back against the barn. He saw Beth making her way along the road toward him. He secretly hoped that one day he could pilot a ship with her aboard. Brushing the dirt from his knees, he stood up and pushed the hair off his face, leaving a streak of dirt across his forehead. He stood still while Beth rubbed the dirt off. He wondered when it would be the right time to kiss her again.

"Want some stew and biscuits?" JW asked. "Ma just made a fresh batch, and I'm going to have some."

"Sure, if there's enough," Beth said.

"There is, but even if not I'd share mine with you." He blushed when he realized what he'd said.

"Aren't you the gentleman," Beth said. John Wallace Donaldson blushed a deeper crimson.

He held the door for Beth as she entered the kitchen, then hurried to the wash basin and washed his hands.

"Hello, Mrs. Donaldson," Beth said. "John Wallace told me you've been busy baking, and he's offered me some biscuits and stew. He even said he would share his with me if there wasn't enough."

"Oh, he did, did he? He must be going sweet on you, dear," Mrs. Donaldson said, and this time it was Beth's turn to blush a little.

JW heard his father stir in his room and lowered his voice. While Beth and his mother set the kitchen table, he went upstairs to get his swimming trunks to take along, just in case the water was warm enough. He'd noticed that Beth had brought her swimsuit.

Stopping halfway down the stairs, JW looked to where his mother and Beth stood. He hadn't realized that Beth was as tall as his mother. It struck him that he and Beth would be in high school in a couple of months and were no longer children.

"Let's get going. Time's a'wasting," JW said after they'd had some stew. "Bye, Ma."

"Bye, Mrs. Donaldson. Thanks for lunch," Beth added.

"Yeah, thanks, Ma."

Chapter 8

Mary felt the strong hand of her husband squeeze her arm as he laid his arm across her shoulders. She smiled sadly as she watched Beth and JW walk away from the house.

"You'd better get some sleep, Andrew dear. You've only been down for a couple hours," Mary said.

"I can't sleep with thoughts of the boy going into that black hole. I keep hoping that work will somehow pick up, but it seems more likely it'll just get worse. Is there any other way?"

"I wish I knew. I'd take in washing to do, but no one can afford to pay to have their laundry done. The few folks that can have live-ins. I can't see any other way but for John Wallace to go to work. When are you gonna tell him?" Mary asked.

"I'm gonna keep drawing the pictures, and I'll start telling him about how coal mining works, and we'll see how it goes from there," Andrew said. "You're right. I better try to get a few more hours sleep," he said, and kissed Mary's forehead before heading to the bedroom.

Chapter 9

July was almost over, and JW's bedroom wall was filling with pictures of the underground workings of the mine. The details of how each part fit with the others in order to ensure safe production of coal were interesting, but JW missed the stories of talking fish and runaway horses and the bones of long-dead animals. But it seemed important to his father that he pay close attention, so he did.

He learned that hard coal, mined in Pennsylvania, was called anthracite and was used largely in homes for heating. He also learned that softer coal, the kind mined in Cape Breton, was known as bituminous. Since there was no known anthracite in Nova Scotia, bituminous was what they used as fuel in their homes. Bituminous was also used in the production of coke and coke was used in the production of steel.

As he put the pictures together on his wall, JW noticed they were forming a mural. It looked like an underground city with men whose blackened faces had a haunted look. Some leading and others following horses along the railway lines. He shivered as he peered into their faces. His eyes were always drawn first to the one that looked like his friend Mickey.

His father hadn't included a picture of the opening where the men went down in the trip to the mine below, but he told him about it. The trip, or rake, as it was also called, consisted of pulley cars that ran on small railway tracks. JW followed the natural progression from start to finish and traced tunnels where men used black powder to blast open new seams of coal, and followed other tunnels that were already in production. Huge timbers had been put in place to support the roof. In other areas, pillars of coal were left to hold up the ceiling overhead. Two-man teams dug out the rooms and loaded the coal.

Their backbreaking work expanded the mine deeper into the earth and even under the ocean.

JW was surprised to learn that once a room was stripped of its coal, the ceiling was collapsed using a pick. The resulting mass of coal was known as a miner's harvest. It was extremely dangerous work and could be fatal. Only the skill of the miner and his wits kept him safe. The harvest was part of his own father's work. Fear entered into JW's heart for his father and for his friend Mickey.

His father stressed the importance of the two shafts that were constructed along the seam of coal. One shaft carried fresh air into the deeps, which was the working face of the mine, and the other shaft carried the stale, gas-

filled air back to the surface. JW learned that canaries, housed in little cages carried on a pole, were used as a warning system to let the men know when the gas levels were dangerously high. If the canaries jumped about or died, then the men knew it was time to leave the area. He learned more than he ever wanted to know, but his father was relentless in his instruction. He told him that a building on the surface housed the fans that blew the air into the mines. He learned that years ago there were furnaces used in the mines to circulate the air, but they were too dangerous and increased the risk of explosions. They were replaced with the fans.

"See here? This is where they extended the mine. The old shaft had to be boarded up to keep the air in. You see there? That's where they cut a hole and put a door so the horses can get through. They call it a trap, a trap door. You open the door to let the horse through, then you close it quickly to trap the air, to keep it from crossing over so it'll be forced down to where the men are working. That's where they came up with the name, trap boy or trapper boy. You understand?" his father asked.

"Sure, Da, I understand," JW said. "But I never plan to go down there."

"John Wallace–" his mother began, but stopped as she caught her husband's look. She saw him shake his head *no*. "Why don't you finish up your breakfast and go fishing for the day? I'm sure Beth will be by soon."

"We're going to go to the fort and read for the day. I still have two whole books left and half of another one to read before school starts back. It's hard to believe summer's half over. If they teach any courses on coal mining, I'll know most of it. Same time tomorrow, Da?" JW asked.

"Same time. Maybe I'll have a funny story to add. We'll see how tonight goes. How's that sound?"

"Just as long as there's pictures," JW said as he left the kitchen table. "See you at supper time." He hurried out the back door and across the field. He wanted to get there before Beth.

Chapter 10

"Why do you figure he's telling you all the stuff about the pit?" Beth asked.

"I don't know, but I don't like the sound of it," JW said as he leaned against the wall of the fort, *The Count of Monte Cristo* propped up on his knees. "It's probably because I've asked for so many stories over the years and now I'm getting older, so he's telling me grown-up stories. It makes me worry for my father and poor Mickey. I just couldn't imagine doing that for the rest of my life."

Changing the subject, JW asked, "What did you bring for lunch?"

"Me? I thought it was your turn to bring lunch," Beth said. "Just kidding." She laughed as she pulled a drumstick for each of them from the basket.

JW could see other goodies in the picnic basket and thanked her as she handed him the food. Finally, when he'd finished the large slab of apple pie, he didn't think he'd be able to move for an hour. Gulliver had fared well also, eating the leftover scraps of chicken.

Beth and JW discussed the first two chapters of *The Count of Monte Cristo* and agreed that it was a great story to get lost in, whisked off to a fanciful time.

Chapter 11

JW listened as his father spoke of the importance of understanding the workings underground. It was mid-August, and although the pictures had stopped, the stories of the pit had intensified. Stories were repeated over and over, and JW was sometimes asked to bring the pictures to the table so his father could point out locations where each job was carried out.

He learned the history of mining, at least the recent history, and how there was a brotherhood among the men who worked underground and how sticking together was crucial to the success of the union.

"Sometimes we hafta to go on strike in order to get better wages and better working conditions," his father said. "Last year's strike took a terrible toll on the men. William Davis lost his life for the cause, being shot by the company goons. There's talk a strike could be just as bad again this year. Roy the Wolf wants to take more from the little wages we're getting now. The Company could end up closing with him at the helm.

"If it hadn't been for our union leaders, especially J. B. McLachlan, fighting for our rights, we'd be working for nothing. He had us stand up to Wolvin last year. It even cost J. B. four months in prison on some trumped-up charge. Wolvin only cares about money. If we don't agree to his terms, he just cuts our hours even more. With the shifts cut to three or four a week, I can't make it on the little that's coming in now, JW." Andrew Donaldson looked into his son's eyes and then looked at his teacup.

"Maybe I can get a part-time job after school, Da. I could check down at the Co-op, see if there's anything there with deliveries after school and on Saturday."

"Mr. Ferneyhough's got two boys working there now, and I heard that a few miners have even approached him looking for work. Before long, with the hours cut back, Mr. Ferneyhough's not going to be very busy either. I wish there was something you could do after school."

"Maybe I could help some people with their gardens?"

"I'm sorry, JW. You hafta go to work. We don't have any other way to get by. I talked to the manager and he said you can start underground as a trapper boy 'cause they don't need any more boys picking rocks at the breakers. It's better pay anyway." Andrew stood up from the table and began to walk outside.

"What? You want me to go in the pit? I'm going to school. I can't go to work there!" JW shouted.

"There won't be any school, John Wallace. Weren't you listening? We've got no choice. My hours have been cut, and if we can't pay the taxes on the house, we'll lose it. The government will take it. Besides, I owe the Co-op most of my pay, and I can't keep running up a bill if I can't pay it."

"It's not fair! I shouldn't have to go in the mines."

"Life's not fair!" His father stared at him. "I pass by lots of boys every day that work at the breakers and others working underground, including Mickey." His father's voice softened. "I wish it wasn't so, but it's all set. You start in two weeks," he said, then went outside.

"We're sorry about your schooling, John Wallace, but we need the money," his mother said.

No school and stuck in the mines forever. He felt betrayed. He rose from the table.

"You can do whatever you want for the next two weeks."

JW gathered the pictures together and moved slowly as he walked upstairs to his room. He laid the pictures on his bookshelf, no longer interested in putting them on the wall, for all too soon he'd be able to see himself alongside Mickey. Tears streamed down his face, and he was overcome by a mix of anger and frustration. He wanted to go to school. He wanted to visit far-off lands.

He lay face down on his bed to smother the sound of his crying and didn't hear his mother come into his room. He felt her hand rest on his back.

"I'm sorry, John Wallace. I know you had your heart set on school. Maybe in a year or two the wages will pick up and you can go back then," she said in a reassuring voice. "Right now your father is working every available hour, and we can't keep up."

"I know, Ma, but once I'm in, I'm there for good," he said. A sudden thought came to mind. "Will I be working the back shift like Da? Maybe I can still go to school and sleep in the afternoon." Sitting up in his bed, he said, "Yeah, that's what I'll do. If all I gotta do is pull the door open and closed all night, then I should be able to go to school too."

JW didn't see the sad look in his mother's eyes as she said, "Well, you can sure give it a try. Why don't you go fishing for the day, or go see Beth?"

"I think I'm just gonna lie here for a while and think about things. Tell Da I'll talk to him later," was the quiet reply.

Chapter 12

"I didn't have the heart to tell him he'd be too tired to go to school after working all night. I don't see the harm in letting him think he'll be able to do it," Mary said. "He seemed to perk up once he figured he could do both."

Andrew rubbed his calloused hands over his face. "Not much chance of that. The poor little fella. He doesn't know the half of it. It's a different life down there. You stop being a boy the minute you go underground. He'll be treated like one of the men, and there's no place for fear of the dark."

Andrew and Mary walked arm in arm toward the barn, each one silently wishing that life was fairer and that JW could remain a child for at least a little while longer. They walked behind the barn and saw the garden. The plants had grown well under their son's care.

"There should be enough potatoes to last the winter," Andrew said. "He worked hard on the weeding. Well, I better get in and get to bed, though I don't think I'll sleep much."

"I told him he could have the next two weeks to do as he pleased," Mary said. They looked at each other and fell silent.

Chapter 13

"You mean you'll be doing the same job as Mickey?" Beth asked.

"Yeah, that's what Da said, trapping," JW said.

"What about school?"

"Oh, I plan to work back shift and go to school during the day and sleep in the afternoon," he said, sure that the plan would work.

"When would you have time to do your homework? Grade nine is not easy, lots of new courses. I hear the math is really hard. Besides, remember poor Mickey. He couldn't keep up, even with you tutoring him," Beth said, not realizing that she was dashing his hopes.

JW felt despair steal into his heart but put on a brave face. "I'll just do it somehow. I got to. Ma said the wages might pick up in a year or so and I'd be able to return full time, so if I can make a passing grade, that'll do."

"When do you start?" Beth asked.

"Just around the time school reopens. I'll work the night before and show up for the first day of classes." He was no longer sure he'd be able to work and attend school as well, but he planned to try. "I gotta get home soon. Ma and I have to go to town to get my work clothes. I guess it can get pretty cold down there, so I'll need some warm clothes."

"Yeah, and pretty dark too," Beth said, and shivered. "I'd be scared to death down there, JW. You are some brave," Beth said, and kissed his cheek. "We better get back then, so you can get your outfit."

Chapter 14

Mary Donaldson talked about their garden, marvelling at the size of some of the plants. "The potatoes grew well, I'm sure there'll be five or more on a stalk, and the corn is taller than your father. He said we should have enough potatoes to do the winter." She asked about the fort and about Beth, never mentioning school or the pit.

JW smiled and nodded in all the right places. However, his heart sank when they passed the high school on their way to the Co-operative. Since the company stores had closed the previous year, the Co-op had extended credit to many of the miners and their families. He didn't understand the difference between the company-run store and the ones run by the merchants but was told the difference was huge.

"We'll get an account set up for you, and each week a part of your earnings will go to pay for the clothes and supplies you'll need. I'll explain to Mr. Ferneyhough that you'll be starting work next week and that you'll be in as soon as you get your pay," his mother told him. She pushed open the door, and the clang of the bell announced their arrival.

JW looked across the bins and saw Mrs. Johnson, his grade-eight teacher, picking up supplies. He smiled and nodded his head as she greeted him.

"Oh hi, John Wallace. Did you have a good summer? I hope you're all rested and ready for high school. We're all counting on you to do wonderfully," she said with obvious pride. "You have a brilliant boy there, Mrs. Donaldson. He should do marvellously this year. Are you in to buy supplies, then?" she asked them.

JW saw the grimace on his mother's face. "Yes, but clothing supplies. John Wallace will be starting in the pit next week. Good day to you, Mrs. Johnson. We have to get along now," Mary Donaldson said, and hurried toward the clothing bin.

"But, Mrs. Donaldson, John Wallace has so much potential. Surely there must be some way that he can go to school," Mrs. Johnson said, sadness now present in her voice. "He can't work in the pit and successfully complete his studies," she added.

Mary Donaldson moved in as close as possible to JW's former teacher. "The pit is filled with boys with lots of potential. We've fallen on hard times and we need the money that John Wallace will be able to bring in. Please don't make this any harder than it already is."

JW turned and nodded to Mrs. Johnson and noticed she was patting her eyes with her handkerchief. "Bye, Mrs. Johnson," he said.

Taking Mary aside, Mr. Ferneyhough spoke in a low voice that was more like a stage whisper. "Now, Mrs. Donaldson, you are behind on your payments already." Holding up his hand, he continued. "I realize it's not your fault and that Mr. Donaldson's hours have been cut back, but–"

"John Wallace will be starting in the pit next week, and he'll be in every week to get us caught up," Mary Donaldson said, her own whisper low enough not to be overheard.

JW stood beside the bin, trying not to look at his mother, whose face had turned a bright red.

Mr. Ferneyhough did an about-face. "I'll be happy to set up an account for John Wallace." Turning to JW, he said, "Once you start in the coal mine, you got a job for life."

The walk home was quiet. Neither JW nor his mother was in the mood to pretend to be upbeat. He hung his new clothes in the closet and closed the door tightly. Thoughts of school came to mind and he picked up the satchel his grandfather had given him so many years before. Picking up the pictures his father had drawn, JW put them inside the empty satchel. He placed a single scribbler and a pencil inside as well and laid the satchel back on his bookshelf. The words of Mr. Ferneyhough came to mind: *Once you start in the coal mine, you got a job for life.* JW said a silent prayer, hoping that Mr. Ferneyhough was wrong, but the words of Mrs. Johnson echoed in his head: *He can't work in the pit and successfully complete his studies.*

JW lay on his bed for a long time. He watched through his bedroom window as the sky turned dark. There were no stars and the moon was hiding behind the clouds. A short while later he heard his father moving around in the kitchen below. In less than a week, he would be down there with him getting ready to go to work as well. He sighed loudly as a hopeless feeling came over him. Stories of the pit no longer interested him. Even the books on his bookshelf no longer held intrigue.

Chapter 15

"Come on, JW, time to get up," his father said, as he shook him gently. "Remember I told you we were going to the mine today to get you familiar with the place. We'll drop by the breakers and see where the coal is screened. That's where the youngsters pick the rocks and shale from the coal. That's backbreaking work. A trapper job is easier on the body."

"Why don't the boys at the breakers do the trapper jobs then?" JW asked.

"They're too young. Some of them are only nine or ten years old and aren't allowed underground."

"Don't they go to school?"

"Not many. Well, let's get moving. As soon as you have a bite of breakfast, we'll get on the road," his father said, and rubbed his son's head.

A quick wash, followed by a bowl of porridge, and JW was ready to go. "Bye, Ma. See you in a couple of hours. If Beth comes by, tell her I'll see her later."

JW ran to the barn and scraped out Lightning's stall. He filled the water bucket and threw some hay in with the horse. "See you, boy. I'll brush you down later."

The walk to the mine was quiet, with few words exchanged between JW and his father. He still couldn't believe that he was actually going to be working there in a few days.

"Are we going down in the pit today, Da?"

"No, just to the breakers. You'll go in the mine on your first shift. That's how it works. We're coming up to the breakers now."

JW stood beside his father and watched as coal on conveyor belts sped toward the boys, who deftly picked rocks and shale from the coal. Their blackened faces and hands disguised their ages somewhat, but their slight stature revealed their true age. *Children. They're just children*, he thought.

The rushing coal had no mercy as it struck the tiny hands of the boys who laboured there. JW was shocked to see that some of the boys were missing fingers and others had fingers bent and twisted.

"Look at their hands, Da," he said.

"I know. Some of them will never be able to go underground as miners. You can't be a pick-miner unless your hands are in good shape. And you can't support a family on a breaker boy wage."

"How come he's getting to go trapping?" JW heard one of the boys ask.

"Yeah, it don't seem fair. He gets to go to a good job," another boy said.

"Hey, you!" a boy called out.

JW turned to where the voice had come from.

"You should have to take a breaker job before getting to go down to the trap. Hope the rats don't eat you, or the ghosts." Several boys broke into laughter. "Yeah, lots of dead miners down there looking for the trap boys that fell asleep on 'em. It's so dark you can't see them coming. Wooo … watch out for the rats." More laughter followed and JW was glad when his father signalled it was time to leave.

"Pay no attention. They're just trying to scare you."

And they're doing a good job of it, JW thought, and felt fear send a shiver down his spine. He wished he could stay on the surface, anything but going down into the darkness.

"Do the rats attack people? Can you see them coming?" JW asked, his fear escalating.

"Like I told you, it's pitch black down there, and you can't see your hand in front of your face. Sometimes your oil lamp burns out before your shift's over. And the rats do come pretty close, but they're just looking for crumbs from your bread."

His father's explanation did nothing to allay his fears, and JW swallowed several times. No further questions were asked, because each new answer made him more afraid.

Chapter 16

"They were like little men. And angry that I was going to be a trapper boy," JW said. He watched Beth's eyes open wide. "Some of them only come up to my waist, but they act like they're bigger than me. After we left the breakers, we walked to where the rake goes down to the mine face, the deeps. The rake is also known as the trip. The entrance looks like a gaping hole in the side of a hill. I would have liked to go down to where I'll be working, but Da said that's not allowed."

JW felt Beth's hand slip into his as they walked along the riverbank. He squeezed her hand and felt it tighten on his. They walked for several minutes without talking.

"If you have to miss some days from school, I'll help you catch up on Sundays."

"That would be great, but I don't plan on missing too many days." This time Beth did not remind him of Mickey and his inability to continue in school.

They left the river and walked through a wooded area that came out on a bluff overlooking the ocean. JW's gaze took in a section of shoreline that displayed black sand. A large seam of coal protruded from the water, and he shivered as he thought about going down into the ground and out under the ocean. Beth slipped her arm around his waist, as if sensing his thoughts.

They stood for a time looking at the water and the whitecaps that danced on the ocean's surface. The churning water matched the turmoil that JW felt. He knew he had to go to work but wanted desperately to attend high school as one of the kids. He wondered if his sense of adventure would be lost forever once he entered into the blackness.

The setting sun spread an array of colours across the horizon in stark contrast to the thoughts running through his mind. It would soon be night, so they'd have to hurry to get home before dark.

"The sun looks nice, doesn't it?" JW said, breaking the silence. "We'd better get back soon, or your ma will send a search party."

"I didn't realize the time. Yeah, we better get on home or Ma just might," Beth said and once again held his hand.

They made good time heading back the way they'd come. Usually they parted at Donaldson's gate, but tonight JW decided to see her home. It was much darker than usual, and he didn't want her alone on the road after nightfall. They reached the top of the hill above Beth's house, and JW released her hand.

"I'll wait here until you get to your door," he said. "Goodnight, Beth, and thanks for a great day." As she smiled, he added, "I enjoyed the whole summer. It was fun fixing up the fort and swimming, but I didn't finish all the books, did you?" JW asked.

"Once I heard you were going in the pit, I stopped reading. I still have several chapters left in the *Count of Monte Cristo*."

"Me too. I thought about all the digging he'd done and it made me think of the pit, so I put down the book. I plan to finish it though. Perhaps it has a happy ending."

Beth leaned toward JW and kissed him. "I had a great summer too. I hope the pit isn't too hard and that you'll be at school most days."

"That's the plan."

"Goodnight," Beth said, and started down over the hill. She walked with purpose and made it quickly to her door. She turned and waved. JW returned the gesture.

Buoyed by the kiss, he thought perhaps they were boyfriend and girlfriend or soon would be. He started on his way home but turned to look at Beth's house. He was surprised to see she was still standing outside watching him. He waved again, and after waving back, Beth went indoors. Twilight had turned to darkness, but the crescent moon guided his way. He heard an owl hoot and picked up his step. The thought of the dark woods increased the beating of his heart. He let out a shrill whistle, and moments later he heard the racing of feet coming toward him. Gulliver bounded along the road, head down, as fast as he could run.

"Hello, Gullie. How's my boy, huh?" JW dropped to one knee to pet him, happy to see his loyal friend.

Gulliver's response was his usual full-body shuffle. He wagged his tail, licked JW's face and barked as if to say, "I'm here to protect you" or "nice to see you." JW wasn't sure which it was, but thought perhaps it was a little of both.

Chapter 17

JW tried to eat some of the stew his mother placed before him.

"You better eat a bit of it, 'cause you'll be awake all night," she said. "Don't want you hungry down there."

He ate a few spoonfuls, but just wasn't used to eating at ten o'clock at night. "I'm trying, but I'm still full from my first supper," he said. Forced laughter filled the kitchen as everyone pretended tonight was like any other night. But it wasn't, because tonight was the first night that John Wallace Donaldson would be entering the mine.

The stew was hot and delicious, but his throat felt as if it was closing in, and he laid his spoon down. He swallowed the last mouthful, aided by his tea.

He'd spent the last few hours lying in his bed, trying to sleep until it was time to get ready. The stars were bright tonight and would keep him company on his walk to the mine. Besides, his father would be with him for the first few nights. Although his father had asked for them to be on the same shift, it would only be for tonight and the next two. BESCO's president, Roy Wolvin, had cut the men's hours so they'd only be working three or four days a week. JW and his father would be working different shifts spread throughout the week.

JW pulled on his coat and reached for his satchel.

"What have you got there?" his father asked.

"My books for school. Tomorrow's the first day," JW answered. "Is there a place to wash up in the morning, or should I come home first to wash?"

"There's a place to wash, but you might be better off coming home first to have some breakfast, so you can leave the satchel till morning. You might be a little tired after your first shift..." His father's voice trailed off.

"I know, but I gotta go on the first day to find out what classes I'll have and who'll be my teachers," JW said. He laid the satchel aside and picked up the lunch box.

"My, look at the time," his mother said. "You best be on your way before you're late." Mary Donaldson kissed her husband and hugged her son.

JW saw the look on his mother's face and tried to re-assure her. "Don't worry, Ma. I'm not scared. Da told me everything I need to know, so I'll be fine."

"I know you will, dear. Just keep your wits about you, and remember to stay awake, 'cause it's an important job you'll be doing," she said as JW and his father went out the door.

"I will, Ma, don't worry."

JW felt something wet touch his hand. He pulled sharply into the path of his father.

"Whoa, it's only Gulliver wishing you goodnight," his father said. They laughed and his father clapped him on the back. Gulliver followed them for part of the journey, but JW thought it best the dog return home so his mother wouldn't be alone. Dropping to one knee, he hugged Gulliver.

"Go on home, boy, and look after things." Gulliver stood for a moment before turning and heading back home.

"I am sorry that you have to go to work. With the hours cut back, there isn't any other way to pay the bills."

"I know, Da."

"It was bad enough when there was the company store. At least we could get our supplies. But many miners, me included, didn't like that most of our pay went back to the company. We thought the strike would give us more money so that if we wanted to we could buy from the Co-op and other merchants. We were on strike for better rights."

"Wasn't it the Premier who sent in the army to keep the men off mine property?" JW asked.

"Yes it was, and it didn't help when Wolvin's right-hand man, Vice-president McClurg, said we'd go back to work on their terms."

"I remember reading Mr. McClurg's quote from the Sydney Post, talking about the miners. 'They can't stand the gaff,' I think was what he said. What did that mean?"

"That's what he said, and it meant they'd put so much pressure on us that we'd give in and go back to work, and that only made the men more determined to stay on strike. The men are still angry over last year's strike, and you can't blame them. The coal company tried to starve us out. William Davis was killed, and the company stores are gone."

"I guess the only good thing that came out of it is that Premier Armstrong was defeated," JW said.

"That, and McClurg leaving Cape Breton. With any luck, Wolvin'll soon follow."

JW felt a little nervous when he realized that they had almost reached the mine.

"You know, the men have a tradition. They let the rake travel faster than usual whenever there's a new man going under for the first time. It's their way of welcoming the man to a new way of life. Actually, it's a way of scaring the good out of a fella. Don't let on I told you, and act afraid," his father said.

"I think I got the afraid part down already," JW said.

"You'll have a fella with you for part of the night, but after that, you'll be on your own. So pay attention to what he says. Not everyone you meet is gonna be friendly, so just do your job and you should get along fine. Okay?"

"Okay, Da."

JW heard the men laughing as he and his father approached. They were talking about dances and card games they'd been to and ones they would be going to. The men stopped talking as he drew nearer.

"Looks like we got some new blood. We got a special seat for you up at the front of the rake since tonight'll be your first trip down the travelling way," a large man said.

JW was glad he'd paid attention to his father's lessons. He knew the travelling way was the tunnel the men and horses used to get in and out of the mine.

His father whispered, "You'll be fine, don't be scared."

"Okay, Da." He wondered why his father didn't ride in the trip with him, but he soon noticed no one took the seat beside him. It was all part of his initiation.

"Keep your head low and hold on," someone said.

The beating of his heart pounded in his ears as the rake started its descent. Soon it felt as if his heart would explode from his chest as the trip picked up speed. He didn't have to close his eyes because the darkness was complete. The blackness was overwhelming and a scream escaped his lips.

JW felt the blood rush to his cheeks as laughter erupted from every man on the rake, except perhaps one. He heard a man say, "Poor little fella. He'll find the time long down there." Another man added, "Too bad about him. He'll learn like all the rest. My boy's been at it for months now, and that's after a couple years at the breakers."

JW recognized the voice of Mickey McGuire's father. He wondered if he'd be working with Mickey, but quickly remembered he'd be alone at the trap door. The sudden stop made JW rise up in his seat and he bumped his head. He refused to call out this time, for he knew more ridicule would follow. He felt his father's hand on his shoulder.

"Remember to keep the flame on the lamp as low as you can, or you'll run out of oil," his father said. "See you in the morning."

The men stopped long enough to light their lamps and were off again. The height of the tunnel was just over four feet, and everyone had to bend to keep from bumping their heads on the beams that supported the ceilings.

Bobbing lights speckled the road ahead of JW until, one by one, they disappeared, and he was alone.

Chapter 18

JW turned around in the absolute darkness. He hadn't gotten his lamp lit before the men left. Where was the man who was to train him? Panic paralyzed him for a moment. He jumped when he heard a sound to his left.

"Just giving you time to get used to the darkness before I take you to the trap," the man's voice said.

"Who are you?"

"Name's Red Angus. You're Andy's boy, aren't you?"

"Yes, sir, I am. John Wallace Donaldson, sir."

"Sir? I've never been called 'sir' before. Just call me Red. That's the colour of my hair. Everyone down here's got a nickname. I think I'll call you JW. Yeah, that's your new name, JW." JW smiled to himself and watched with relief as Red pulled his oil lamp from underneath a wooden box, the wick turned so low that the flame was barely visible.

"I just wanted you to see how dark it really is down here," Red said as he turned up the wick, and a small ray of light illuminated the area around them. "I'm gonna spend a couple of hours with you until you get the hang of the door. It's not hard, but sometimes it gets sticky, so you gotta pull real hard on the rope. I s'pose Andy's told you about how important it is that the trap door is closed, to keep the air in?" Red Angus asked.

"Yes, sir," JW said.

"Red Angus, or just Red'll do. Okay, JW?"

"Yes, s– Red Angus."

"Pass me your lamp, JW. I'll get her lighted up for you."

With his lamp lit, JW felt some of the tension leave his body. He could see his surroundings a little better than with just Red's lamp. They walked for ten or fifteen minutes before Red said they'd reached their destination.

"Trap boys are the first in the mine and the last out, 'cause you control the air. We just gotta wait here until the horse and tram comes along, then I'll show you how the door works."

Within a half hour, Red announced that it was time. JW watched as Red pulled the trap door open, and the horse and tram, led by a miner, made their way through. The trap door was immediately pulled closed. He watched closely as Red showed him the counterweight on the door. He learned that he had to pull the door open with the rope and then let go of the rope. The counterweight would pull it closed.

"Be sure to give the door a push to make sure it's closed all the way."

"I will."

A short while later, JW heard the approach of another horse. The bobbing light of the miner's lamp illuminated the horse's face somewhat, and JW thought of how his father referred to their horse as a beast of burden. *What a terrible existence*, JW thought. He stood ready, waiting for Red's instructions.

"Get ready," Red said. "Wait'll he gets a little closer, then pull her hard."

"Yes, Red," JW said. He stood poised to pull the door.

"Pull her now, JW."

JW pulled the door and was relieved when it slid open. Once the tram cleared the doorway, he let go of the rope and watched the door close, then pushed on it, as he'd seen Red do.

"Good job, JW. Good job," Red said. "I'll watch you do another two and then leave you to it."

JW had been starting to relax, but felt his heart rate quicken at the thought of Red's leaving. The two oil lamps cast enough light for JW to take in his surroundings, but the area was far from bright. Water splashed beneath his feet each time he took a step. Overhead, a small trickle dripped a few inches left of the door, which he assumed accounted for the water that accumulated underfoot.

Movement crossed his line of vision, and JW followed the shadow with his lamp. He drew in a breath at the sight of several rats scrambling over each other. *Gee, they're big*, he thought to himself and shivered.

"Here comes another. You do her all this time," Red said.

JW swallowed and noticed his mouth was dry. He stood ready, but before he pulled the door open, the miner leading the horse called out.

"Hurry, boy! Open her up. No time for lollygagging down here. Time to grow up, boy."

As he drew nearer, JW looked into the face of Mickey McGuire's father. He pulled open the door and stood aside, closing it as the cart cleared the doorway. From the

other side of the trap door, he heard: "Careful, boy! You almost hit the horse."

JW felt Red's hand on his arm.

"Don't pay any attention to Shawn McGuire, JW. He's angry at the world. I'm surprised young Mick is as friendly a lad as he is. But you did good. Pulled the door at the right time. Just remember, there's a lot of nice fellas down here, but not all the fellas you meet are friendly-like."

JW nodded and remembered his father saying something similar. As long as they weren't mean, he didn't care if they were friendly.

"You ain't sixteen yet, are you?" Red asked.

"Not yet, Red."

"Your Pa musta signed a paper like Shawn did for Mick to get you underground. Years ago, kids as young as six and seven were trap boys, but they changed the age to go underground back in 1923. Now they say you gotta be sixteen before going in the pit."

JW knew his parents must be pretty desperate if they had to seek permission to get him the job. "I don't know. All I know is I'm here now." If he'd been able to wait another three years, he would have completed grade eleven. Perhaps the economy would have been better and he could have stayed in school. JW pushed the thought from his mind.

"What time do I finish up in the morning, Red?"

"You'll be heading for the surface about six-thirty," Red answered. "Why?"

"Tomorrow's the first day of school, and I was wondering how much time I'll have before classes start."

"Can't see you being able to work all night and attend school all day," Red said.

"I have to finish high school if I'm ever going to get to college. I don't want to spend my life underground. Not that there's anything wrong with the work. It's just that I want to travel, you know, explore the world." JW stopped talking, because he felt embarrassed. His dreams sounded silly, even to himself.

A chill had set into his bones and he shivered. The thought of spending his life in these mines was suffocating, but very real. Water splashed as he stepped toward the door. A few drops reached his lips; the taste was metallic and gritty. He heard a horse whinny and readied himself at the door.

"If you get this one okay, then I'll be off," Red said.

JW pulled the door open and watched as the miner struck the horse hard in the ribs to get him to move faster.

"Hey!" JW said.

"Shh..." Red said. "Mind your business."

The horse plodded its way through the doorway, and JW closed it as soon as the tram cleared.

"He shouldn't hit the horse like that," JW said.

"You're right. But if you say anything to him, it might be you he hits next. Most of the horses get treated better than the men, 'cause it don't cost nothing to get men, they're free. But the horses are owned by the company, and they had to pay for them. They get the best of food and water, and the lodgings ain't too bad either, if you don't mind bunking down with rats."

JW shuddered and turned his lamp in the direction he had seen the rats. They were still there.

"You're a quick learner, JW, so I'm gonna head back to the surface. You got your lunch with you, so you can eat whenever you feel like it. Just be ready to open the door at all times," Red said.

JW asked Red the time before he left. It was only two o'clock, almost five hours before the end of shift. He watched as Red's light moved away from his area.

"Oh, Red, what about the toilet? Where's it at?" JW asked.

"All around you. Cat sanitation," Red said.

"Cat sanitation?"

"Yeah. Just cover up your business like a cat does," Red hollered as he turned down a tunnel, and his light was gone.

JW felt his stomach rumble and was glad his mother had packed him a lunch. He hadn't thought he would get hungry, but he was. He remembered his father telling him to hold the corner of his sandwich with two fingers, and to throw the remaining crusts to the rats.

The strawberries he'd picked in the summer tasted delicious as he swallowed a large bite of his jam sandwich. A few bites later, he was down to a small piece of crust, which he threw toward the place he had last seen the rats. The tea was cold, but it helped wash down bites of the molasses cookie. He took a large bite and felt his fingers touch his lips. He spit some of the cookie at his feet and heard the rats scurry toward him. He threw the remainder back along the track and heard the rats splashing in the water in their bid to be the first to reach the food.

He quickly closed his lunch box and stood next to the door. Suddenly, he felt something move across his feet and a small scream escaped his mouth. He was glad he was alone, so no one could hear him. Moments later, small feet made their way up his pant leg. JW jumped up and down and slapped his leg, but the rat continued to climb inside his pants.

JW undid the top of his pants and reached inside. Grabbing the rat's tail, he flung it toward the wall and heard a loud smack, followed by a pain-filled squeal. Immediately, he wished he hadn't thrown it so hard. The forceful pounding of his heart echoed loudly in his ears, and he leaned back against the wall.

Against advice and better judgement, JW turned up the wick on his lamp. Although the light was only marginally brighter, he felt a little better being able to see his surroundings. Squeaking and squealing noises seemed louder, and JW angled his head toward the rats. Some of them stood on their back legs and sniffed the air, unconcerned by the light. He noticed one rat dragging its injured leg and again wished he hadn't thrown it so hard.

A horse's whinny and then a gruff "get up now" told JW it was time to open the trap door. He stood at the ready and hoped it was one of the friendly miners, who could dispel the fear he was feeling.

"Long night, eh, lad?" the miner asked as he passed through the doorway.

"Yes, sir, it is," JW answered. As he let the door close, he heard the man call out.

"Best turn..."

The rest of the words were muffled as the door closed. JW listened as the horse and cart sounds became fainter. He wondered what the man wanted to tell him, then realized he had left the light on his lamp turned up. Grudgingly, he turned the light down, and once again the darkness encroached on the space that had been dimly lit.

Two more drivers came through before Red Angus appeared to tell him he had completed his first night. His eyes felt droopy as he followed behind Red. The blackness and absence of time was unnerving. JW knew the rats had helped keep him awake.

"You made her through the night, JW," Red said. "So it's off to home and bed for you."

"I'm off to school for the day, Red. Like I said earlier, it's the first day of school. I'll go home and have a quick wash before I go."

"You'll need more than a quick wash from a night below. You don't have to handle coal to get dirty down here. The coal dust'll do that to you."

JW put his hands in front of his lamp and saw they were filthy. Soon they were standing with the other men, waiting for the trip to take them to the surface. He stood quietly and felt exhaustion wash over him. A strong hand squeezed his shoulder.

"Hi, JW. Got any stories to tell?" his father asked.

"I've got a few," JW said. Some parts of the stories he would keep to himself.

His father grinned. "You can wash up here. That way you'll be ready for school on time."

"I don't have soap or towels with me."

"I brought towels and a change of clothes for you with me last night. They're up top with mine."

The uphill ride to the surface was slower than last night's descent. There was no one to scare this morning, and most of the men were too tired for pranks. Within the bathhouse, a large pipe drilled with holes splashed water over the men. JW watched as his father took a spot next to another man.

All of the men's faces were as black as the coal they mined, and their bodies matched the colour. JW was surprised to see that the coal dust had blackened his body as well. Taking the soap his father had given him, JW stood beneath the water and tried to wash away the night's dirt.

It was seven-thirty by the time they headed toward home. The warm September morning drove away the chill from the pit. JW learned that he would wear his regular clothes to the pit, and change into his work clothes, which were left at the mine. He would take them home weekly for washing and mending. He told his father about the rats and the one that had gone up his pant leg.

"Oh, I forgot to tell you to tie off your pant legs. We'll make sure you do that tonight."

"I did some scrambling and dancing with that in my pants. But I threw it against the wall, and it seemed like it hurt its leg," JW said.

"A lot of men hit them with their shovels because they're just as afraid of them as you are."

JW couldn't imagine killing the rats that were only seeking food, but if they crawled up his pant leg again, he might reconsider his beliefs.

The walk home was fast. Gulliver ran to meet them and was pleased to see his young master. His nose tapped against JW's hand as he sought to be petted.

Fried eggs were waiting for JW and his father when they got home, and he realized that his mother had to collect the eggs this morning. With him in the coal mine, extra work fell to her. Coal and kindling were beside the stove. With the thought of entering the pit for the first time, he had forgotten to get it in last evening.

"Hi, Ma. Porridge would have been fine," JW said, as he dropped into a chair.

"You're a working man now, so you need a big supper," his mother said.

JW was used to calling his father's morning meal "supper," but it was the first time for him. He ate his food quickly and was back on the road toward school by twenty minutes past eight.

Chapter 19

When he reached the hill above Beth's house, JW saw she was waiting for him.

"How was it? Were you scared? Of course not," Beth said before he had a chance to answer. "So tell me, how was it?" she asked again, excitement present in her voice.

"Well, there's lots of rats down there, and they sure are hungry. One near ate my leg," JW told her, watching as Beth's eyes opened wide.

"Near ate your leg?" Beth said and waited.

"Well, not really. But one did crawl up my pant leg. I'll be sure to tuck my pants in my boots tonight and tie a string around them."

"Is it very dark underground? What do you have to do?" Beth asked.

"It's dark as pitch, but the oil lamp helps a bit. I have to control the air in the tunnel by opening and closing the trap door. So you have to be ready when the horses are coming through," he explained. "I met a nice fellow. Red Angus is his name. He told me everyone in the pit has a nickname. He gave me one."

As they walked, he looked at the sun and realized how lucky he'd been before entering the pit. The air smelled fresher, and he paid special attention to the birds singing.

"Well, are you going to tell me your nickname, or is it a secret, some kind of code?" Beth said, smiling at him.

"JW," he said.

"What?" Beth said.

"JW. That's my nickname."

"Pretty much everyone calls you that," Beth said.

"I know that, but he doesn't."

The schoolyard was filled with students, many of whom were returning for their second and third years. A large group of grade nine students stood off to one corner of the yard. He and Beth hurried over.

JW listened as Beth told some of the other kids that he was working in the mine. There were some sad faces as his friends digested the news. He hoped classes would soon begin. He was tired from standing around, especially after spending all night on his feet. The ringing of the bell was music to his ears, and he joined the crowd as they shuffled toward the double doors that led to the high school.

Orientation took twenty minutes, followed by English class. JW listened with interest to the poetry and paid close attention to the titles of the books he would have to read throughout the year. French class seemed like a continuation of last year, building on grammar and conversation.

When the final morning class arrived, JW felt his eyes closing against his will. Trying desperately to remain alert but losing the battle, he thought the algebra being taught seemed to him like a new language. Finally, the bell rang for lunch, and he sought out Beth.

"I can't stay any longer today. I'm just too tired. I practically slept through algebra. If you could pick up my other books and assignments, I'll get them from you later," he said, as a face-altering yawn overtook him.

"Sure, I'll drop them off to your house right after school. Tell your mother I'll be over," Beth said, squeezing his arm.

JW walked to the office to speak with the principal.

"I hope you don't plan on making it a habit to come half days, because it won't be long before you've fallen far behind your classmates," Mr. Morrison said.

"No, sir," was the reply. "Last night was my first night in the pit, so my body hasn't made the adjustment yet. I hope after a few nights, it will get used to the switch between nighttime and daytime."

"Okay, son. Go home and get some sleep. I hope to see you back here tomorrow. If you can't make it every day, come as often as you can," Mr. Morrison said.

JW thanked him, pleased to learn there would be some leeway regarding his attendance. He hoped his body would adjust quickly to being awake nights and sleeping days.

The walk home was brutal, his legs and feet tired from standing for too many hours. JW felt the last of his strength leave his body as his feet hit the front step of his house. Draping his coat over the stair post, he waved to his mother as he went upstairs to his room. He laid his books and satchel on the shelf. His head hit the pillow, and sleep followed immediately.

Chapter 20

"John Wallace, time to get up," his mother called from downstairs.

"I'll be right there, Ma," he answered, and jumped to his feet. He knew he wouldn't have much time to get his school work done before work. He dressed quickly, pulling on the clothes he had worn to school. He would change into fresh clothes in the morning when he got home.

The clock began to chime as he gathered up his books and satchel. He counted the number of chimes, and his heart sank when he heard nine of them. JW had asked his mother to wake him at eight, so at least he'd have close to two hours to do some of the work and check out the books Beth had brought for him. He hoped she'd remembered to bring them.

"Ma, I had to get up at eight."

"You were sleeping so soundly, I didn't have the heart to wake you, dear."

"It's the only way I'll be able to keep up," JW said. "I have to get up early. Well, I'll really have to study fast and hard tonight."

"Come and have your breakfast with your father," Mary Donaldson said, and headed toward the kitchen.

"Can I eat in the dining room, so I can look over my homework?" JW asked. The dining room was usually only used for special occasions like Christmas and Easter.

"I'll bring in some stew for you," his mother said.

"Thanks, Ma." Pulling open his math book, he scribbled what he remembered from class, something about finding the variable for X. Using the examples from class, he quickly understood the concept and breathed a sigh of relief. Moving to English, he found the poetry was familiar and broke it into the required rhyme scheme. Lying on the table were three more books Beth had delivered for him. Inside the top book, she had written out his class schedule. Two subjects didn't require assignments, but a chapter had to be read for science. He noticed his science class was right after lunch, so he would browse through part of it now and finish it at lunch tomorrow.

The stew was hot and good, and he made sure to eat extra bread. He figured the more food he ate, the more energy he would have and the less likely he would be to fall asleep.

"C'mon along now," his father said. "We gotta get moving."

"Be right there, Da." He pulled on his coat and kissed his mother's cheek. "See you in the morning, Ma."

Rushing outside, he hurried to the toilet, and then to the barn where he shovelled out the stall. He threw in some hay and a handful of oats for Lightning. "I'll brush you down tomorrow," JW said as he petted him.

Gulliver stood at his side waiting for his turn to be petted. JW bent down and hugged Gulliver to him. "You look after the house now, boy."

"We gotta get moving," his father said again.

"Coming now, Da," JW called out, and hurried to catch up with his father, who had started down the road. He knew his father wouldn't leave without him, but he understood that they had to leave right away, or they could miss the trip.

"What are you taking with you?" his father asked.

"My satchel, the one Pa made."

"I wouldn't leave that up top. Could be gone by morning."

"I'm gonna take it to the trap with me. I even got my lunch in it."

"It's gonna get awful dirty underground."

JW pulled something from his pocket. "I took an old pillow case to wrap it in down below."

"Alright, that might do the trick."

The walk seemed a little hurried, but he kept pace with his father. "How far are you from where I'm working, Da?" JW asked. He waited, wondering if his father had heard him.

After almost a minute had passed his father said, "Less than a quarter mile, probably half that. If you followed the horses that you let through and walked past the first three tunnels, I'm in the next tunnel, about three hundred yards in. You'd know it right off, it's the one with all the water in it. Before long, they're gonna hafta close her down, or it might come down on its own."

"You think there's any danger of that happening?"

"Sure, it could—" his father said, then realized he was scaring him. "But the sky could fall, and I don't expect that to happen anytime soon. How did school go today?" he asked, steering the conversation in a different direction.

"Pretty good. I could only stay until lunchtime though. I thought I was gonna fall asleep on the way home. Beth brought over the rest of my books. I spoke to

Mr. Morrison, the principal. He seems good. Said I was to come whenever I could."

"Ah, that sounds fair."

The rumble of voices meant they had arrived. JW spotted Mickey up ahead and caught up to him.

"Hi, Mickey," JW said. "You working tonight?"

"John Wallace Donaldson! I never thought I'd see you down here! I heard you screamed like a girl on the trip last night."

JW felt the heat rise to his face. He hadn't cared that the miners had heard him, but Mickey knowing he'd screamed was embarrassing.

"But don't worry, I did the first time. Most of them did too," Mickey said, waving his arm to take in all the men waiting for the trip. "That's why they do it to all the new kids, so that someone else gets laughed at for a change."

JW was relieved to hear he wasn't the only one who had screamed. "I'll see you later, Mickey," he said.

—

Andrew Donaldson listened to JW and Mickey, as Mickey explained that everyone was scared the first time down the trip. But Andrew knew different, because he had been one seat behind Mickey, who hadn't made a sound his first night going below. *What a kind boy,* Andrew thought.

Chapter 21

The descent was slower than the night before and without incident. Mickey took a seat next to JW, and they laughed on the way down. Red met them once the trip stopped.

"I'm just gonna walk with you, JW, and make sure the door's opening proper," Red said.

"I didn't see you get on the trip. What do you do, sleep down here?" JW asked with a laugh.

"Sometimes."

The walk along the travelling way didn't seem as frightening tonight. JW struck up a conversation with Red, asking him about family.

"Nah, I never had time to get married and have kids. But I live with my sister and her husband, and they got a couple of boys, so I get to take them fishing," Red said.

"I caught a big one a few weeks back," JW told him. "He was as big as my forearm, from my elbow to the tips of my fingers." He held out his arm in the darkness.

"What was it, a codfish?"

"No, a trout."

"Musta been some eating on that one, JW," Red said.

"I was holding him in my hands and he snapped his tail, hit the bank, and was back in the water in a matter of seconds, but—"

"It sounds like a 'one that got away' story. You've only spent one night underground and already you can spin tall tales," Red said, chuckling. Before JW could respond, Red added, "Well, we're here."

JW looked at the trap door and felt a shiver run the length of his spine. He watched Red pull a stick slathered with grease from a bucket beside the door. The bucket was hidden in the shadows, and JW hadn't noticed it the night before.

"You plaster it on the hinges every second night, and it makes opening it a whole lot easier. The door's heavy and you don't want it sticking," Red said, as he liberally spread the grease.

JW paid close attention. "So every second night, Red?"

"Yeah, that should do," Red said. "I see you came down on the rake with young Mick tonight."

"We spent six years in school together, before he came to the pit."

"Well, you'll get to spend the next forty or fifty years together down here," Red said, not realizing the feeling of despair his comments had stirred in JW. "I gotta get over to feed the horses," he said, pulling the trap door to make sure it opened easily.

Chapter 22

Alone in the darkness, JW turned up the wick on his lamp and saw long shadows on the far walls. Rats stood on their hind legs as if in a macabre dance. He watched as several sniffed the air. JW noticed the one with the injured leg kept to the back of the pack. He knew the rat wouldn't last long because the healthy ones would get to the food first.

JW rubbed his hand along the wall and felt a small indentation he'd noticed the night before. He brushed aside some loose shale and the opening grew larger. He continued to pull shale and small rocks aside until there was just enough room to fit his satchel in the hole. And the hole was high enough off the ground that the rats couldn't reach it.

The familiar sound of metal against metal told JW it was time to move nearer to the trap door. As soon as the horse came into view, JW pulled the door and it opened smoothly.

"Might be an hour or more before the next cart comes through. There's been a small collapse back a ways, and

it's gonna take some time to clear it from the track," the miner said.

"Is everyone okay?"

"Oh yeah, just dirt on the track."

"Thanks for letting me know," JW said. He waited until the cart cleared the doorway then closed the door.

He decided to have some of his lunch while he waited. He reached deep into his satchel and pulled out a molasses cookie. The rats squealed as they sensed the food. He ate all of the cookie except for the small portion that rested between the coal-stained fingers of his right hand. He reached his left hand into his satchel and his fingers closed around what he sought. He walked a few steps and threw the remaining piece of cookie as far as he could into the darkness.

JW watched as the healthy rats scurried after the morsel, their shadows moving hurriedly in his lamp's light. The injured rat tried in vain to follow, but soon stopped. JW walked toward the injured rat and watched as it tried to get away. The rat pulled its wounded leg behind itself, but made little progress. Stopping a few feet from the rat, JW opened his hand, letting the oats fall to the floor. He then backed away, and watched as the rat greedily ate the meal. It was able to consume most of the oats before the other rats returned.

"Boo!"

JW jumped and felt his breath whoosh from his mouth. He managed not to scream.

"You're easily spooked for an underground miner," Mickey said, unable to hold in his laughter.

JW angled his lamp so it illuminated Mickey's face. "I wasn't expecting any visitors, especially not ones that tap you on the shoulder and shout 'boo.'"

Mickey continued to laugh, and JW soon joined in.

"Did you hear there was a small cave-in and that there won't be any trams through for an hour or more?" Mickey asked.

"Yeah, I heard. Well, at least I got the rats to keep me company."

Mickey reached to pick up a lump of coal. "Just throw something at them and they'll stay away."

"No, don't do that. I already hurt one last night. I made the mistake of dropping some food at my feet, and one of them was up my pant leg before I knew it. I threw it against the wall. Poor thing, it was only looking for food."

"You got your pant legs tied up tonight?" Mickey asked.

"Yeah, I won't make that mistake again."

"You know the best thing when there's a cave-in? I mean when no one's hurt, of course. You get to go exploring 'cause you don't have to worry about the door. It just stays closed."

"Da said I wasn't to leave the door under any circumstances," JW said.

"That's what every new man is told on the first shift, but after a while, you get to realize that it's okay to do a little exploring, as long as you're here when the trams are ready to go," Mickey said. "I do it all the time. C'mon, I'll show you where your father works. I'm working the door close to where he is." Mickey pulled a rock from his pocket. "Look what I found on one of my treasure hunts."

"What is it?" JW asked and squinted in the dull light. He saw a fossilized imprint of a dead animal. At least it looked different from the usual ferns and other plants. Perhaps it was a fish.

"I'm not sure, but there's a bunch more in the same tunnel. It's only a five-minute walk up the tracks. We can be up and back before they even think of getting the cave-in cleared."

Against his better judgement, JW ignored his father's warning and decided to follow Mickey. It was just a short distance, and they'd only be gone a few minutes. It felt like old times – Mickey and him on a treasure hunt.

Mickey pulled open the trap door, and for the first time JW ventured beyond it. He watched Mickey pull it closed and waited until he took the lead. Their headlamps cast a dull light. Mickey walked the tram rails as if he'd been doing it his entire life. JW looked up the tunnel that Mickey pointed out as the one JW's father worked in. It was dark and he couldn't see any light at all.

"It's just up ahead where I found the rock I showed you," Mickey said. "The tunnel has lots of other strange-looking rocks in it too."

"Is it a working tunnel?" JW asked.

"No, it's abandoned. There was a cave-in months ago, and Old Man Hennessey was hurt real bad, so they closed it down. We gotta be careful, walk lightly."

Entering the tunnel, JW felt a shiver run across his shoulders and wondered if he should turn around. The promise of long-dead animals encased in stone and coal overruled his fear. His father had told him and Mickey many times about the fossilized animals and plants found at the Joggins coal fields on Nova Scotia's mainland. A famous scientist, Charles Lyell, had discovered them there many years ago.

"A few more feet and we'll be there," Mickey said. "Look!"

JW stared at the pile of rocks and saw the outline of something. Pulling a piece of coal closer to his face, he was disappointed to see it looked like the skeletal remains of a plant, perhaps a fern. He dropped it and pulled another from the pile. It also looked like a plant of some kind.

"Are these the only rocks you found?" JW asked.

"There's more in further, but it's too dangerous to go in any deeper. But it's where I found this rock," Mickey said, holding it out. "You can have it. I can get more later."

"No, that's yours. I mean, thanks, but I want you and I to find some more on our next treasure hunt."

"We better get back," Mickey said. "There'll be a lot of trouble if we're not at our doors once the trams start running again."

Mickey pointed the way to JW's trap door, then turned to go back to his own.

"Can't you walk back with me?" JW asked.

"You're not afraid, are you?"

"Not really, but I don't want to get lost."

"Just follow the tracks back to your door. You can't get lost," Mickey said.

"What if the trap door won't open from this side?" JW asked, unable to hide his rising panic.

"Alright, I'll walk you back."

"Thanks."

They walked in silence. JW felt the blood rise to his cheeks and stay there. He waited until Mickey pushed on the door and then slid through the opening.

"Thanks, Mickey."

"Sure, no problem."

They heard the sounds of metal against metal and knew that the trams were running again.

"Oh no! I'll never get back to my door in time," Mickey said, and broke into a run.

With the door opened a crack, JW watched for a moment as Mickey hurried along the tracks. The tram was already making the turn, so JW closed the door tightly. He attempted to make small talk in order to slow down the miner.

"I've no time to talk, boy. Worked all night with nothing to show for it. Open the door, boy."

JW pulled the rope and watched as man and beast sped along on their journey, coal dust falling from the cart. He closed the trap door again, and soon the silence returned, broken only by the occasional squeak of a rat.

JW hoped Mickey had made it back to his door before the unhappy miner. His face flushed hot at the memory of Mickey walking him back to his trap door. Fear of the dark had overwhelmed him. He recalled the pleading that had been in his voice and the reluctant agreement of Mickey. Few words had been exchanged.

He had little time to think about much of anything, because several minutes later another pony came pulling a filled cart. A short time later it was followed by another, and JW listened to the familiar sound of metal on metal.

He realized the extra carts must have been the ones waiting on the other side of the roof-fall.

JW leaned his back against the wall and felt something move across his boot. His heartbeat quickened. Pulling his foot back, he saw it was the lame rat. His first instinct was to shoo it away, but instead he reached into his coat pocket and found a few oats. He let them fall next to his foot. The rat devoured the oats and scurried into the darkness. It wasn't ready to trust him completely.

He leaned against the wall again, and his heart beat slow and regular. He felt his eyelids become heavy, and stood up straight. After a few minutes, his eyes again started to close, and he shuffled his feet, but sleep overtook him. He awoke to the sound of bells ringing softly. A miner stood before him, and the horse, with bells connected to his harness, shook his head from side to side. The bells reminded JW of a sleigh ride he'd been on years earlier.

"You find the nights long, do you, son?" the man asked.

"Yes, sir, I do," JW answered.

"They surely are. I spent a year on this very door, and many a night I drifted off to sleep. But I somehow got used to it. I was about sixteen when I started in the mine. Have to keep your mind filled to stay awake on this job. I did a lot of daydreaming. Thought about places I'd been before coming underground and wished I was back there. Still think about the ships I sailed on from time to time. The ocean can be a terrible master, but to see the sun in the day and the moon and stars at night … ah, those were fine times. My name's David Smith, but folks call me Smitty."

"Mine's John Wallace Donaldson, but some call me JW. Where did you sail on the ships?"

"Back home in Barbados," Smitty said.

"Barbados. That's in the Caribbean, right?"

"It sure is, and the water is as blue as the sky, and the sand is as white as snow. But the promise of a job that would give us a better life convinced my family to move here ten years ago. Lots of men from all over the world came to work these mines."

"My friend Frankie, I just found out his father works down here. They came from Italy," JW said.

"Yes, and Janus, who now goes by John, brought his family here from Poland. We all came hoping to escape poverty only to find it seems to have followed us," Smitty said.

"I would love to sail a ship to Barbados some day. Do you plan to return there?"

"Perhaps one day. Maybe on a ship when you are the captain." They both laughed. "Better get the door open, son."

Pulling the door open, JW listened to the bells and remembered the sleigh ride as he watched Smitty go through. He hoped that he could learn more about Barbados. Perhaps he could learn from the other men about their countries as well.

Chapter 23

Mary Donaldson turned quickly in response to the knocking at the back door, her hand coming to her mouth, surprised to see Beth standing in the doorway.

"Come in, dear. What brings you here?" she asked.

"Good morning, Mrs. Donaldson. I thought I'd meet John Wallace this morning and walk with him to school."

"Won't he be surprised then?" Mary said.

"I don't know how he can do it. Staying up all night and then half of the day," Beth said.

"I know, dear. I'm worried he's not getting enough sleep. He says he wants to spend an hour or two on his studies every evening. If he does that, he'll only be sleeping five or so hours a night. He won't be able to keep up the pace."

"He hopes work picks up at the mine and that maybe he'll be able to return to school full time," Beth said, her eyes hopeful.

"I know what he hopes for, Beth, but I've never seen the mine in this shape before. The owners don't seem to care if the men and their families starve. It takes John Wallace and his father both working just to bring in enough to manage. If his father was still getting five shifts a week then John Wallace never would've had to go to the pit."

Gulliver's barking drew a halt to their conversation. Beth watched as Gulliver raced down the road. She heard the shrill whistle of JW.

"I'll wait outside until he's eaten," Beth said.

"I won't hear of such a thing, and I'm sure John Wallace wouldn't either. Sit right at the table and I'll pour you a cuppa tea."

Beth sat and waited. JW's eyes lit up when he saw her at the table.

"Is everything alright?" he asked.

"Yes. I came to walk to school with you," Beth said. "You are going, aren't you?"

"I sure am. After I have a bite of breakfast, I'll be ready to go. I finished all my homework. I just want to read the science chapter again."

"Yeah. I read it a few times before it made any sense. We can talk about it on the way to school," Beth said.

Mary watched the two children discussing their studies. Her smile was sad, for she believed they were heading in opposite directions. Still, she hurried them along so they would not be late for class.

"Come right home after school, John Wallace."

"Oh I will, Ma. If not before," JW said, and put his hand up to stifle a yawn. He looked at Beth and his mother. "Once I get used to the shifts, I'm sure it'll get easier."

"Come again any time, Beth," Mary said.

"Thank you for the tea."

Chapter 24

"The numbers inside the brackets are...." Mr. Cantwell's voice became a droning sound, the words no longer discernable, as JW fought against sleep. It wasn't quite eleven o'clock, and he had nodded off several times. Each time he awoke, Mr. Cantwell was further along in the lesson. JW stared at the numbers on the blackboard and realized he could no longer follow the teacher's instructions.

Raising his hand, JW asked to be excused. He packed his scribbler and textbook into his satchel and left the room. A few muffled voices reached his ears: "He should be home in bed. He can't handle it." He tried to ignore the comments but knew the others were right. Trying to do work and go to school was beginning to look impossible. During the walk home, JW's mood changed from negative to positive to negative again as he tried to decide what he should do. Entering his home, he waved a hand to his mother and went upstairs to bed.

He wondered if he shouldn't just give up on the idea of going to school. It would make life easier if he could just come home from work and sleep away the day. JW's mind raced. There was so much to consider, but his tired body was telling him to take it easy. Lying on the bed, JW was set to give up on school until he looked at the picture his father had drawn of his friend Mickey. The haunted eyes seemed to be pleading for escape. Perhaps he would try again tomorrow.

He slept fitfully; rats chased him down the darkened tunnels, and Mickey laughed at him, telling other men that JW had always been afraid of the dark. Angry men yelled for him to hurry and open the trap door. His father joined in with the men, laughing and laughing … JW woke and pulled the blankets up to his neck. He wondered if he'd called out. He hoped he hadn't. He didn't want his mother to know he was afraid. But the darkness.... He fell back to sleep. This time he didn't dream.

Chapter 25

"Come on, dear," Mary Donaldson called from the bottom of the stairs. "It's time to get up now."

"Okay, Ma. Be right there." He wanted to turn over and go back to sleep but knew he had to get up. He looked around for his satchel, but it was nowhere to be seen. Panic-stricken, he knelt down and looked under his bed. It wasn't anywhere in the room.

"Ma. Did you see my satchel?" JW asked as he ran down the stairs.

"It's on the table. I went up and got it earlier and set your work out for you. There's a bowl of beans ready for you and a cuppa tea. I'll feed your father a little later on. Hurry on then. Get to your work."

JW looked at his mother. "Thanks, Ma. I'll get right at it." He opened his math book and read the pages he had slept through in class. After a few minutes he caught on to the lesson. He read several pages further and tried a few more questions. The hours passed quickly.

"All right then, JW, it's time to go," his father said. "Best pack up your bag."

"Yes, sir." JW packed his school books and the lunch his mother had made in his satchel. He noticed a large supply of kindling by the stove and saw that the coal bucket had been filled. He didn't like the thought of his mother having to get in the coal and wood.

"I'm sorry, Ma. I forgot about the coal and kindling."

"Don't worry about it, dear. Your father got it in this morning."

Relieved, JW hurried into his coat and boots and hugged his mother. He went outside and petted Gulliver then rushed in and cleaned out Lightning's stall. He threw in some hay and oats, pocketing a handful of oats for the injured rat. From beside the barn, JW saw his mother silhouetted in the doorway and watched as his father bent to kiss her. She was a strong woman who stayed alone at night. He was glad she had Gulliver there to protect her.

JW crouched beside Gulliver and whispered for him to guard the house. He waved to his mother as he hurried to catch up to his father. Starting tomorrow, he would have to make the trek by himself. He was scheduled to work, but his father had the next two days off. The mine's owners had cut the hours, and his father was to lose two full shifts this week. The only reason JW was working every day was because there was coal to be hauled from the mine face, and someone had to be there to open and close the trap door.

"Finding it tough to stay awake in school, are you?" his father asked.

"Yes. I'm ready to go after breakfast, but by eleven o'clock it's like someone's pulling on my eyelids trying to make them close. Sometimes I wake up and I've missed half of what the teacher has said. I don't know if I'll be able to keep going or not."

"Time will tell," his father said, then changed the subject. "Do you remember what I told you about the workings of the mine? How the whole process works from start to finish?"

"I sure do, Da."

"Start at the beginning and tell me what it takes to get the coal to the surface."

"Once the seam has been discovered, they use black powder to blast the new tunnel, and then they divide the tunnels into exact sizes. Room and pillar is where the shafts of coal are left to support the roof. The part I don't like is the miner's harvest. It seems terribly dangerous for a man to pick at the ceiling until it falls to the ground. Why do they take the chance?" JW asked.

"It's because the coal is right above you for the taking. There's tons of coal available. It's a chance for the men to make a decent day's pay. You just got to keep your mind on the task at hand, and when you hear it getting ready to let go, run like the devil."

JW spent the rest of the walk explaining how the coal got to the surface, and his father seemed pleased that he understood how the process worked.

"I carry the pictures that you drew," JW said, tapping the satchel. "So if I get rusty on the details, I'll be able to just look at them and remember."

JW took notice of the graveyard as they neared it. He hadn't thought much of it until that moment, when he realized he would have to pass it alone tomorrow. "I wonder if Gulliver could walk with me tomorrow night? You know, to keep me company."

"I don't think that'd be a problem. I'm sure old Gulliver would like the exercise," his father said. "And I'll be home to be there with your mother. Watch where I put

our clothes tonight, so you'll know where to put yours when I'm not with you."

"Sure."

As JW and his father arrived at the mine, he heard some of the men grumbling about the reduced hours and the loss of wages. His father joined in, but JW stood back. It was adult talk, and besides, he would have been quite happy to be off work the next couple of days to get caught up on school. At least next week he would only have to work three days.

Mickey stood behind his father but didn't say anything as the men continued to discuss the lost wages. JW waved to him and received a slight nod in response. He wondered if Mickey was angry because of last night. JW was still a little embarrassed about asking Mickey to walk him back to his door. The rake started loading and JW hurried to get a seat. He was surprised when Mickey took a seat next to him.

"I thought you were mad at me about last night," JW said in a low voice.

"Nah," Mickey said. "I still don't like the dark either. I was lucky to get back before Old Man Reilly got there. Boy, is he cranky. Makes Da seem timid." They both laughed at this, because Mickey's father was anything but timid. "Whatcha got in the satchel?" Mickey asked.

"My lunch and school books," JW said.

"School books? You mean you're still going to school?"

"I get about half the day in before I have to go home, but next week I'll only have to work three days, so I hope to get at least two full days in. My marks won't be as high as I'd like, but even if I can get a pass—"

"Didn't you hear? One of the trapper boys broke his leg playing ball and won't be working for a month or more. You and I'll be here at least five days a week, maybe more," Mickey said.

JW felt the trip come to a stop at about the same time he felt his hopes vanish. He knew there was no way he could work five or six days a week and keep up with his school studies. He wanted to cry, but didn't.

"I hope you're wrong."

"I wish I was, but Red told me last night. He said there were some changes coming soon too. Something 'bout a new man in charge. I'll see you later if I get a chance."

JW lit his headlamp and walked to the door. He pulled his satchel off his shoulder and wrapped it in the pillowcase, then laid it on the ledge where the rats couldn't reach it. Before long, he heard the scraping of a coal-filled cart, and got ready to open the door. It was Old Man Reilly. JW pulled the door open just as Reilly seemed ready to say something.

"Good evening, sir," JW said.

"Hrmph," Reilly responded in an unintelligible mumble.

JW closed the door and reached for the grease to lather the hinges and then realized they had been greased the night before. He crossed the tracks and stood by the ledge where his satchel was resting. His mind raced at the prospect of having to spend six nights a week in this darkness.

Before long another cart arrived. This time he heard bells announcing the arrival and was happy to see Smitty.

"You look wide awake tonight, JW. Did you get some sleep?"

"Yes, a little. It's still early though. I'm usually good until halfway through the night," JW said. "I heard there are some changes coming, a new man in charge?"

"I know that Red is finally retiring. He's an overman. You know, a boss. He keeps the shifts running pretty smoothly. They're gonna have to look long and hard to find another man who knows all the workings of the mine. Better open up the door, JW, or I won't earn any pay tonight."

JW was surprised to learn that Red was a boss. He imagined that a boss would holler a lot, but Red had been quiet and kind. Something moved across his boot, and JW saw the injured rat and forgot all about Red retiring. He dropped a small pile of oats and watched as the rat ate a little more slowly. It seemed to linger a moment after it was finished, perhaps beginning to trust him. He watched as it made its way across the tracks and into a dark corner. It no longer seemed to be part of the pack. JW knew how it felt, alone in the dark.

The rest of the night passed without incident, and JW was glad when he saw the men heading toward the travelling way. He hurried behind them before realizing he'd left his satchel on the ledge. He turned and started to run back to his trap door. He'd have to hurry or he'd miss the rake and be down there for hours. As he rounded a turn, he bumped into his father.

"This what you're looking for?" his father asked, holding up the satchel.

"It sure is."

"It's kinda heavy. What've you got in it?"

"School books and the pictures you drew."

"Why not leave the school books home until morning?"

"Just in case I have to work a little later. I could go right to school from here."

His father smiled. "We best get along then. How was your night?"

"Pretty good, Da. Mickey said that a trapper boy broke his leg playing ball and will be off for a month or more and that him and me will have to work five or six nights a week. I hope that's not true."

"We'll talk about it on the way home," his father said. "Okay?"

"Sure."

The water streamed over them and washed away some of the night's dust and grime. JW was trying to process all that he had heard: working six nights a week, Red quitting and a new boss being needed.

The sun was bright as JW and his father went outside. Some young boys were throwing rocks at crows that had perched on the wires beside the breakers. The crows were there hoping to scavenge a few morsels from the men's lunch pails; the boys were passing time until their shift started in the breakers. The crows dodged the rocks thrown by the boys, who would soon be dodging shale and coal that came crashing down the chutes to maim or dismember them.

"Tough night?" JW asked, noticing his father's shuffling gait.

"Yeah, I loaded a lot of coal and pulled down a room last night. The roof didn't seem to want to let go. I musta swung the pick a thousand times before it finally dropped. I can't say I'm sorry I'm not working tonight."

"What?" JW asked, then remembered he'd be making the walk alone.

"As you know, I'm done for the week now. I was talking to Red, and he told me about needing you to work. I told him you'd be there."

JW looked at the large trees that lined the road to home and remembered last night how the branches had appeared to be arms reaching out toward him. He shivered.

"I'll walk partway with you tonight," his father said, and JW relaxed a little, having expected Gulliver would be his only companion. It would be his first night underground without his father. He hoped he could be brave. JW suspected the men would taunt him because of his father's absence.

"I worked three so far, so how many more this week?" he asked.

"It seems like you might have to work right through till Saturday," his father said.

JW looked down at the dirt road and kicked at a stone, watching as it rose into the air before falling into the field. He didn't bother complaining, because he knew the money was needed.

"Did you hear Red is retiring? He said he's gonna take his nephews fishing a little more often. Maybe do some travelling. You know, he spent close to fifty years in the pit. That's longer than I am old," his father said.

"Yeah, if I stay underground that long, I'll be sixty-three," JW said.

They walked the rest of the way home in silence. JW picked at his food, then left the table to go upstairs.

"Do you want me to pack you a sandwich for school?" his mother asked.

"I'm not going today. I think I'm going to get some rest if I've got to work the rest of the week. I just want to sleep all day. Goodnight, Ma, Da. I'll see you tonight."

—

Mary Donaldson watched her son trudge up the stairs and turned to her husband. "It's tearing the spirit from him, Andrew. Like he's lost or something. I can hardly bear to watch him looking that way."

"It was only a matter of time before he'd hafta give up on school. It just came sooner than later. If he don't work the extra shifts this week, they'll get rid of him," Andrew said. "I'm gonna lie down for a few hours, then I'll see if there's things that need fixing."

Mary sat at the kitchen table and wondered what would become of her son. His dreams, she knew, had never included the coal mines. The only tunnels he'd have imagined would have hidden treasures in them.

Chapter 26

JW awoke. It was bright outside. He listened for a moment and heard a light hammering and assumed that was what had awakened him. Turning to face the wall, he felt sleep's embrace welcome him again and soon his chest rose and fell rhythmically. He dreamed of the pit but not of being chased by rats or being lost in tunnels....

"Hello, John Wallace," Red said.

"Hi, Red. Most everybody calls me JW. I heard you'd retired."

"Not yet. Soon. They're still waiting to replace me."

"Da said you'll be hard to replace."

"I don't know about that, but they need a man who knows the workin's of the entire mine," Red said, and walked through the door, light swinging at his side as he disappeared around a bend in the tunnel.

—

JW awoke and sat up in his bed, remembering Red. The dream was already fading from his memory, but JW wrestled with it and was able to remember the essence. Someone knowledgeable was needed to replace Red.

Getting up from his bed, JW pulled open his satchel. A light dusting of coal covered the pictures his father had

drawn. He opened his bedroom window and blew on the pictures, sending the dust outside. Once they were clean, he laid them out on his bed. The pictures showed every facet of the working coal mine, including the trapper boys. He looked at the trapper boy in the picture and looked into Mickey's haunted eyes. JW wondered if his father had meant to capture that expression on Mickey's face.

It was twilight and he realized he must have slept close to ten hours. The thought of going alone to work filled him with dread. He dressed quickly and headed downstairs. The clock's chimes tolled six times – he had more than three hours before he had to go to work. JW listened to his mother singing in the kitchen. It was a beautiful Irish song, and the lilt in her voice amazed him. He wondered what her dreams had been as a child and planned to ask her that very thing, but when he entered the kitchen, she turned quickly toward him.

"Supper's ready on the stove. The kindling and coal is in for the night. Lightning's stall has been mucked out and he's fed, so you have almost four hours before you have to head off to work. I know you might not be able to keep going, but I want you to at least give it your best attempt before quitting," his mother said. "At least finish out the week."

"I missed today's classes, so I don't know what to do," JW said. "But I guess I could read a couple of chapters in my science book."

"Your father had to go into town to pick up supplies at the Co-operative, and on his way back stopped into the Jessomes.' Beth wrote out what you missed today. Your lessons are on the table."

Seeing the smile in his mother's eyes, he was overwhelmed by her thoughtfulness. "Thanks, Ma, that's a big help. I might as well finish out the week like you say." The meal was dished up before him and JW was surprised to see it was rabbit stew, his favourite. "Gee, Da must have been really busy. He even took time to get a rabbit for supper."

"That was me, dear. I have a couple of snares set behind the barn. The weather's getting colder and there was some frost on the ground yesterday morning, and I saw some tracks, so I set two snares. There was a rabbit in one of them this morning."

"Wow! Not only the cook but the hunter too." They both laughed at this.

The next few hours flew by, and JW managed to do some algebra, science and English, glancing as well at a few passages of French. Once nine o'clock came, his mind began to wander and he could no longer focus on his school work. The thought of going underground without his father was almost paralyzing. Pacing between the kitchen and dining room, he felt his fear heighten.

He walked outside and noticed a chill in the air. It was early for it to be this cold. Indian summer was a ways off yet. He couldn't imagine what it would be like once winter came, walking through banks of snow twice daily if he wanted to stay in school. He pushed the thought to the back of his mind. There was no use worrying about winter, because he still had to get through the next couple of days. If he made it through and continued on, he would worry about it when the time came. JW walked to the barn and petted Lightning, then slipped a handful of oats into his pocket. He hurried to the outdoor toilet and heard the door to the house open and close.

"Where's Da?" JW asked his mother as he washed up, readying himself for the coming walk to the mine.

"I just heard him go outside. He never sleeps much the first night after back shift. Red told him he'll be going days the next couple of weeks."

"Days! I won't be able to go to school if I have to work days."

"Not you, dear. Just your father. You'll be making the walk by yourself most nights, I'm afraid. I can walk part way with you if you want."

JW felt his face flush with embarrassment. His mother was willing to walk him part way to the mine because she knew he was afraid. "No, that's not necessary. Thanks, Ma, but I'm not afraid. I might bring Gulliver along for company, but I'm not afraid," he said, hearing himself repeat it for the second time.

"I know your father plans to walk part way with you tonight," his mother said.

"No, he doesn't have to. I might as well get used to it on my own. Like I said, Gulliver will keep me company. Da can get some rest." JW looked at the clock and made ready to leave. After putting his lunch inside, he slipped the strap of his satchel over his shoulder. "I'll see you in the morning. Porridge will be great. I don't really like eggs all that much, so you can save the eggs for Da or yourself."

"Be careful, and make sure to stay awake. Are you sure you don't want me or your father to walk with you?"

"I'm positive, Ma, thanks. Goodnight."

The moon was almost full, lending a welcome light to the night. JW looked up and noticed there were several clouds overhead. He hoped they didn't drift in and cover the moon. He startled at his father's voice.

"Ready to head into work, JW?"

"Yeah, I guess it's time. The moon's nice and bright. Goodnight, Da," he said and began his walk.

"Hold up. I said I would walk in with you the next couple of nights."

"Thanks, Da, but I might as well do it on my own right from the start. I'll take Gulliver with me part way," he said. "Thanks for getting in the coal and kindling."

"It's only right with me being off the next few nights. Are you sure you don't want me to walk in with you?"

"Pretty sure. Come on, Gullie. You got a long walk ahead of you." JW waved to his father and picked up his pace. With Gulliver at his side he felt unafraid, but that quickly changed when he neared the graveyard. There had been an old church on the property; it had burned down years ago. No one seemed to care for the cemetery anymore, but the trees had not encroached on the graves, which left the markers clearly visible in the moonlit night. Many were lopsided, but a lot were upright. There was a light breeze moving through the leaves and JW's imagination began working overtime. It sounded as if someone was whispering, then he heard a toneless whistling sound. He pulled his satchel to his chest, and briefly considered running home. Instead, he began walking faster toward the mine. He was ready to run when he felt a hand on his shoulder and, for the third time in a week, a short shriek of fear escapes his lips.

"Whoa, JW. It's only me," his father said. "You dropped your lunch. I tried to catch you, but you were moving like a deer. Didn't you hear me whistling at you?"

"Oh gee, Da, you frightened the life out of me. I heard whistling, but it was just when I reached the graveyard, and I figured the ghosts were out to get me."

Both he and his father burst out laughing at the seriousness of the statement.

"I might as well walk the rest of the way with you."

"You better, 'cause it'll take the rest of the way before my heart'll stop racing." JW took his lunch and put it in his satchel, noticing that he hadn't fastened the latch earlier. The black, gaping hole of the mine soon came into view and JW and his father stopped walking. There were several men milling about and their voices carried on the breeze. Girls and dances seemed to dominate the conversations.

"I better walk the rest of the way by myself, or it will only give them something to tease me about," JW said.

"If you think it best," his father said.

"Yeah, I do. Night, Da. Take Gulliver along with you too."

"Night, son. Try to stay awake. Here, Gulliver!"

JW watched for a moment as Gulliver and his father headed toward home. He turned and went to meet up with the other men. He was glad to see Mickey was already there, but he was surprised to see another boy there as well. JW recognized him as one who had been working as a breaker boy. He was the one who had done all the talking, trying to scare him about ghosts.

"Hi, Mick," JW said.

"Nice night, JW," Mickey answered. "This here's Patty. His da signed papers for him to start in as a trap boy beginning next week. He's so anxious he wants to go down tonight for free. Looks like we may not have to work six days a week after all."

"That sounds good. I thought you weren't allowed to go in the mine until your first night underground?" JW said.

Patty moved closer to JW. "Mind your own business. I been working around here for four years and I'm the same age as you."

JW saw that the men had suddenly taken an interest in the three boys. "I just thought it was some kind of rule that you couldn't go underground until your first shift," JW said in a low voice.

"I told you, it's none of your business," Patty said loud enough for all to hear. "If you keep talking …" Patty raised his fists. "I heard you screeched like a banshee the other night, calling out for your mama."

"Stop it, Patty," Mickey said.

"It was your pa that told me, Mick," Patty said. "Do you have to protect him? Can't fight his own battles?"

JW watched in amazement as Patty continued to shout. The men were drawing closer. JW knew there would be trouble. *Perhaps Patty thinks I don't want him working in the mine*, he thought. He watched as Patty pushed past Mickey with his fists raised. He saw the punch coming but reacted too slowly. JW rubbed his cheek where Patty's blow had landed.

"Aren't you gonna fight back, or are you a coward too?" Patty said, smiling for all the men who cheered him on.

Patty's smile changed when JW raised his own fists. He was tired of the laughing from the men, and he surely wasn't about to let a boy his own size laugh at him. As JW moved forward, Patty moved back, suddenly unsure of what to do next. JW's punch to the stomach doubled Patty over, and the one that followed to his cheek knocked him to the ground. The men were no longer cheering. A few pointed at Patty, and some started to laugh. Patty rose to his feet and ran toward JW. After a brief struggle,

JW put Patty in a headlock and they went together to the ground.

"I'm willing to call it a draw," JW whispered in Patty's ear. "We'll just get up and shake hands and that'll be the end of it."

Patty continued to struggle, trying to get free. JW squeezed harder, and Patty stopped moving about.

"Okay, let's call it a draw," Patty said.

"What's going on here?" Red shouted as he approached the boys, who were now standing. "I'm not gonna stand for any foolishness. What are you doing here anyway, Patty? You don't start until next week. Get on your way home."

JW watched as Patty shuffled his feet in the dirt, embarrassed at losing a fight he had started, and then further embarrassed by Red.

"It's my fault, Red. I was showing him some wrestling moves," JW said. "Patty was telling me he's been working here for the last four years. He said he's anxious to learn the ropes on the trap job, so he'll be ready to go next week."

"Yeah, Red, I'll take him with me if that's alright," Mickey said. "He knows most of the stuff anyway. I'll just show him how to grease the hinges and how to open and close the door."

"Okay then. But keep an eye on him, Mick. I wouldn't let this happen normally, but I got so much to do.... And no more wrestling."

Chapter 27

"C'mon, JW, it's Saturday. You can take a few hours away from school work," Mickey said, excitement in his voice.

"I don't have any money to spend on the streetcar. Besides, I got a lot of homework to catch up on," JW said.

"Patty's uncle's the operator, and he'll let us on for free. Patty already asked him."

"Are you sure?" The thought of riding on the electric tram from Sydney Mines to North Sydney was pretty exciting. It had been a few years since he'd been on the streetcar with his mother.

The downtown of Sydney Mines would be bustling with activity in a couple of hours, with shoppers picking up their needed supplies. The approaching winter had the potential to be long, hard and cold. Staples like sugar, flour and vegetables that could be stored in root cellars were commodities that would go quickly; hoarded by some and shared by others. JW was glad the majority of potatoes, turnips and carrots from the garden were already packed away in their cellar. He had spent part of his summer weeding, and the harvest had taken days to complete. There were still some potato and turnip plants to be harvested, but his father would do that before the frost came.

"Here it comes, JW!" Mickey shouted. "Hurry."

The satchel slapped against his side as he hurried to catch Mickey. The streetcar came to a halt, the metal wheels screeching as it stopped. JW noticed there were only a few people on the electric tram, and they were sit-

99

ting close to the back. He listened as Mickey spoke to the operator.

"Morning, Long Jack. How you feeling?"

"Morning, Mick. Back's a mite stiff first thing in the morning, but least I can walk and sit in this seat a few hours a day. Hoping to get back in later on. Who's that with you?"

"Andy's boy, John Wallace. He's trapping same as me. Patty said we could catch a ride up to North Sydney."

"Mighty generous of him," Long Jack said and smiled. "Hop on."

As JW got on the streetcar, Long Jack told him to say hi to his father. Sitting down beside Mickey, JW said, "I didn't know you knew him."

"Oh yeah. Long Jack worked down below until a cave-in three months ago. He's about the tallest under-ground miner I ever saw. Hurt his back in the cave-in. Hard enough to work down there if you're healthy, but with a sore back, it ain't likely he'll ever return."

JW moved from side to side checking out the stores and buildings on each side of Main Street. The post office was huge, the closest thing he'd ever seen to a castle. The top of the building looked like a defensive wall, with gaps spaced every two to three feet where archers might stand to protect the town from invasion or where guns could be fitted to do the same. He could see the ocean off in the distance and dreamed of being on the water. Smitty had told him of the white sand in Barbados and the deep blue water of the Caribbean Sea. He hoped one day he would see it himself. As he looked out at the Atlantic Ocean, he thought he could see white caps on the dark choppy water.

The town was beginning to come to life, and the horses and wagons slowed the speed of the streetcar. JW saw Beth and her parents in one of the wagons. He leaned his head back and thought about school and the coal mines, but mostly he just thought about Beth.

Chapter 28

JW threw a crust of bread down the tunnel then let some oats drop near the grease bucket. He watched as the injured rat drew near, its limp not nearly as bad as the previous night.

"Here you go, Lord Tennyson," JW said, naming the rat after one of his favourite poets. "Eat your fill, but do it quickly, for the pack will soon return."

"Who are you talking to, JW?"

JW turned and saw that Smitty had arrived with a loaded tram. He hurried to the door. "I'm sorry, Smitty. I didn't hear you. What happened to the bells?"

"I forgot to put them on tonight. But with the squeals from the tram, I didn't think I could sneak up on a dead man," Smitty said, laughing. "So who were you talking to?"

JW felt his face flush. "I was talking to a rat. I hurt him the other night, so now I feed him. I named him Lord Tennyson," JW said, becoming more embarrassed as each word left his mouth.

"After Alfred, Lord Tennyson? Why him?"

"Yes. There's a poem I like by him, called 'Tears, Idle Tears.'"

"That's one of my favourites as well," Smitty said.

JW nodded politely. He doubted that anyone working in the mine knew poems by Tennyson or anyone else. He was not prepared for what came next.

"*Tears, idle tears, I know not what they mean, / Tears from the depth of some divine despair / Rise in the heart, and gather to the eyes, / In looking on the happy autumn-fields, / And thinking of the days that are no more.*" Smitty saw the look of surprise on JW's face. "I can see why you'd like that one. There's another that would fit quite well: 'Ask Me No More.' There's a couple of lines: '*Yet, O my friend, I will not have thee die! ... Ask me no more: thy fate and mine are sealed*'."

JW listened in amazement then watched as Smitty clucked his tongue and set the horse on its way through the trap door.

Chapter 29

"I told you about Smitty being from Barbados. Well, I learned last night that his parents were teachers there but decided to bring their family here for a chance at a new life. He was reciting poetry from memory as if he was reading my mind," JW said.

"What do you mean?" Beth asked.

"Remember the rat, Tennyson, I told you about?"

"Yes."

"Well, Smitty recited parts of two Tennyson poems that spoke of the rat's and my fate being sealed. And that was what I was thinking at the time."

"You think that your fate is sealed?"

"Kind of. Tennyson and I are both stuck in the mine, and neither one of us had any say in the matter. Tennyson is stuck because of being born there, and I'm there because of being born into a coal-mining family – our fates are sealed." He stared at Beth with a look of acceptance in his eyes.

"When you're older, you'll be able to leave," Beth said, trying to encourage him.

"Perhaps, but if I work in the mine for the next ten or fifteen years, it'll be too late to try to get an education. The pit will be all I know. Smitty's been there since he was sixteen and he's still there."

Beth looked into JW's eyes and was saddened by the look of resignation. "How is Tennyson's leg?" she asked, trying to lighten the conversation.

"It seems to be healing nicely. He hardly limps at all, but he no longer seems to be part of the pack. I feed him oats when I'm working. I'm surprised someone, or one of the other rats, hasn't killed him. There's no place for weakness in the mine."

The two began walking faster. "Do you think you'll be able to stay for the whole day today?" Beth asked.

"I gotta try or Mr. Cantwell will think I dropped out of science class and won't let me write my exams." They continued talking, and thoughts of the coal mines vanished as the schoolhouse came into view.

The morning passed quickly, but as noontime approached, JW felt his eyelids wanting to close. Placing the math book inside his satchel at the end of class, he caught up with Beth.

"I think I have to go. My eyes are closing."

"You could have a nap here, and I'll wake you after lunch," Beth suggested.

JW's first thought was to say no, but he decided to give it a try. He laid his head on the desk, and after a few minutes felt sleep overtake him.

Beth stood in the doorway for a moment before pulling the door gently closed behind her. She sat on the stairs leading to the first floor below. She took a sandwich from her lunch box and began eating, planning to spend the next hour keeping watch on the door to the classroom where JW slept.

He awoke with a start, his hands reaching for the rope to open the trap door.

"JW," Beth said. "It's time to wake up."

Chapter 30

"John Wallace! I thought you got lost," his mother said as he came through the door. "You better hurry off to bed. It's almost four o'clock and you've got a long night ahead of you. Do you want me to wake you early?"

"No, Ma. I better get all the sleep I can. I managed to stay at school for the whole day. I'll tell you about it later," JW said as he started up the stairs.

He pulled off his clothes and climbed into bed. But the welcoming arms of sleep eluded him, and he tossed and turned side to side. Thoughts of schoolwork and Beth and the dark mines ran through his mind. The daylight outside his window turned to twilight, then darkness. Finally, sleep came.

—

"Wake up, dear. I left you as long as I could. As it is you'll have to eat on the run."

JW opened his eyes and looked into the face of his mother. "Alright, Ma. What time is it?" Just then the chimes of the clock rang ten strikes of the hammer.

His mother called to him as she started back down-stairs. "I'll dish up your meal, so hurry along now."

JW reluctantly got up from his bed and pulled on his clothes. He splashed some water on his face and hands and trudged down the stairs. He ate the food his mother had dished up and turned down offers from his parents to walk with him. He noticed the coal was in and that a large stack of kindling was piled neatly by the stove. Gulliver seemed to be waiting for him as he stepped into the cool night air.

"C'mon, Gullie. Walk me to work, old boy."

Gulliver came to his side and wagged his tail and most of the rest of himself as well. JW started on his way down the road when he remembered he hadn't cleaned Lightning's stall. He turned and rushed toward the barn.

"Whoa! Where you heading?" his father called out.

"I forgot to clean the stall, Da."

"You're the working man right now, so I did it earlier."

"Sorry, Da. I'll get up earlier next time to get it done before I leave."

"You don't hafta do that, JW. It's only right that I do it, that way you can get a little more rest. Besides, with me working days, I've time to get the chores done after work. You best get on your way. Have a safe night."

"Thanks, Da. Goodnight." He made a mental note to try and do some of the chores, but with schoolwork, the mine and sleep, he didn't have much time left in his day.

Gulliver bounded along beside JW, seemingly oblivious to the turmoil going on in his master's mind. He felt JW first slow down then speed up as they neared, then passed, the graveyard. The lights from the mine's opening cast a dull beam on the road in front of them, and the men's voices could be heard.

"Thanks, Gulliver. You go back now and take care of the folks." JW bent down and petted Gulliver's head and shoulders, hugging him. "Go home now, boy. Run along."

Chapter 31

Mickey climbed into the seat beside JW, and Patty got into the seat behind them. Patty seemed nice enough and was full of stories.

"Red said I can go down again tonight. That way I'll be ready when I start on Wednesday."

"Did you see any ghosts yet?" JW asked. "Any rats attack you?"

"Whaddaya mean?" Patty asked, his eyes wide with fear.

"You should know. It was you who told me to watch out for the ghosts and rats. Remember the day I was here with my father?"

"Gee, I was only trying to scare you," Patty said.

"They only come visit you on your first night alone. The ghosts, I mean. The rats are there all the time. But you're lucky, you've been around for a long time, so you won't be afraid when something crawls up through the tracks and grabs you by your leg. Nope, you won't be afraid." JW saw that Patty looked pretty much the way he had felt when the breaker boys had ridiculed him. He didn't like how he'd felt that day, being teased, so JW said, "Just kidding about the ghosts."

"Yeah, I knew you was just pulling my leg, right? Right, Mickey, JW was just pulling my leg?"

"Sure he was. There ain't no ghosts down there, at least none I seen, but there are lots and lots of rats. Some big enough to carry off your lunch box," Mickey said.

"I don't mind the rats. If they bother me, I can just whack 'em with my shovel," Patty said.

The rake started on its way and a low squeal came out of Patty's mouth. It was not as loud as on his first night, but still too loud. He coughed quickly to cover up the sound, but some of the men heard it and a few chuckles rang out.

Chapter 32

"You seem to be pretty comfortable with the trap now," Red said from the darkness.

JW jumped and turned to face Red. "Yes, sir, but I don't think I'll ever get used to voices in the dark. If I keep the hinges greased like you showed me, it seems to open easily."

"I noticed Patty sat right behind you and Mickey tonight," Red said. "I also heard a little squeal out of him. It's not so funny when the shoe's on the other foot. Well, at least with him on the schedule, you'll be able to have a couple days off. I'll make sure Patty gets put on your door when he's ready. How's school going? You'd probably make a good teacher. Patty sure seemed to learn a

lesson after the 'wrestling' match the other night. He's a lot less talkative."

JW looked at Red and realized that he knew it had been more than a wrestling match. "Yes, well, it's good if someone can learn. He seems like a pretty good fellow. Have you decided when you'll be leaving?" he asked.

"No, they still haven't hired anyone, so I guess it could be another month. Are you still in school?"

"Yes, but I mostly only go for half days. I stayed all day today, so I didn't get as much sleep."

"It's hard to burn the candle at both ends. You gotta get enough sleep. Good luck with your studies," Red said and headed through the door. "I'm going to drop in on Mickey and Patty to see how Patty's getting on."

As soon as Red left, JW heard the bells from Smitty's tram.

"I didn't want to sneak up on you tonight, so I put the bells back on," Smitty said. "I'm going on days for the next couple of weeks, so I won't see you for a while."

"At least the bells would keep me awake. If you're going to be on days, do you think you could feed Tennyson?" JW asked and then reached for his satchel to get some oats.

"I got lots of oats, and I'd be happy to feed the old boy," Smitty said. "Well, if I don't see you for a while, take care."

"Bye, Smitty, and thanks." The chiming of the bells made JW think of Christmas, which wasn't that far off. He knew that exams weren't that far off either.

The rest of the night was quiet, and JW felt sleep overtake him on several occasions. He awoke with a start only to find Red standing next to him.

"I'm sorry, Red. I didn't mean to fall asleep. I just nodded off for a minute. It won't happen again," he said, hoping he wasn't about to be fired.

"The nights are long. You woke as soon as I got near you, so I know you would have heard a tram. I was watching Patty, and I think he's ready to go. So you can go to school today and take tonight off and Patty'll work the trap for you. I'll give Mickey tomorrow night off, and Patty can work for him."

"Thanks, Red. I won't close my eyes for the rest of the shift."

"It's just about quitting time anyway, so you might as well pack up. I'll see you at the rake," Red said, and went on his way.

JW reached for his satchel and pulled out some oats to feed Tennyson. He threw a crust of bread up the tracks and the rats scurried after the crumbs. Tennyson made his way over and sat by JW's boot waiting for the oats. JW dropped a small amount and watched as Tennyson devoured it.

"You'll have to hide tonight, because Patty'll be scared of you." JW realized that Tennyson would probably come over to Patty thinking he would feed him. He heard Mickey and Patty talking on the other side of the door and quickly laid open his satchel and watched as Tennyson climbed in searching for more food. JW closed the satchel and felt the slight bulge move inside. He was glad there were lots of oats in there. Tennyson quickly settled in and began to eat.

"Hiya, JW," Mickey and Patty said in unison.

"Hi. Well, let's get going," JW said and pulled the satchel to his side. He held it close as they walked to the trip.

"Whaddaya got in there?" Patty asked.

"Mostly school books, and I use it as my lunch box," JW answered.

"He's got other treasures in there too," Mickey said. "His grandfather made it for him, didn't he, JW?"

"Yes, he did." JW thought of the treasure he had in there now. He saw Red standing by the rake. Red sat beside Patty on the way to the surface. JW watched as Patty nodded his head up and down in response to Red's questions. He was glad to have the night off. He hung the satchel on a hook where he could see it and, entering the wash area, quickly scrubbed the dirt away. He dressed and retrieved the satchel. Tennyson was quiet.

"Thanks, JW," Patty said.

"What for?"

"Red said you didn't mind me having one of your shifts to get started," Patty said.

"You're welcome. I'll see you tomorrow night. Oh, and the rats won't bother you if you throw a piece of bread up the tracks."

"If they come near me, I'll hit 'em with the shovel," Patty said. JW believed he meant it.

Feeling Tennyson move, JW said goodbye to Patty and hurried toward home. Gulliver met him part way, and JW petted his head, keeping the satchel lifted in the air. Gulliver sniffed the bottom of the satchel and whined, curious at what was in there. As they neared the house, JW told Gulliver to stay and went to the barn. He glanced behind to make sure Gulliver stayed by the house.

The musty smell of the barn struck him as he pulled open the door. He heard a soft whinny from Lightning and then a thump as the horse pulled a hoof across the planked floor. JW walked to a corner and knelt down. He opened his satchel, and Tennyson crawled out onto the dry hay. JW watched as Tennyson shuffled forward, his limp much better. He stopped and turned back toward JW.

"Go on, Tennyson. This is your new home. You're free."

Tennyson seemed to pause for a moment then was off again, vanishing into the hay. JW hoped he'd adjust to his new surroundings. He picked up the satchel, petted Lightning's withers, left the barn and walked toward Gulliver, who looked anxious.

"Come on, boy," JW said, slapping his hand against his leg. Gulliver bounded over to his master. JW squatted down and hugged Gulliver to him; for Gulliver, all was right with the world.

———

Andrew Donaldson watched in silence as JW knelt on the floor of the barn. He was about to call out to him when he saw the rat crawl from the satchel. His listened to the soft words spoken to the rat, and was overwhelmed by his son's tenderness. He stayed in the shadows until JW left the barn.

Chapter 33

Mary Donaldson watched John Wallace's head bob toward his porridge. Every few seconds, he would snap his head back and sit up straight in his chair again.

"Are you ready to go? You better hurry or you'll be late. I'm sure Beth is waiting for you," she said.

At the mention of Beth's name, JW stood up and walked to the kitchen sink. He splashed a small amount of water on his face and shook off the sleep that was threatening to overtake him. He brushed off the knees of his pants and ran his fingers through his hair. "I'm ready,

Ma. I'll see you later. I plan to sleep all day and night after I get home. See you, Da. I'll get some coal in when I get home."

"Don't fret about that. I'll have the coal and kindling in. I'm sure I can even get ole Lightning's stall cleaned out. All you gotta do when you get home is sleep." Andrew Donaldson saw the relieved look on his son's face. "Run along and catch up to Beth. You don't want to keep a lady waiting."

JW blushed and saw his parents smiling at him. He couldn't keep from laughing. "You're right, Da, mustn't keep a lady waiting," he said, and hurried out the door.

Chapter 34

The wind had picked up, and JW thought he felt some droplets of rain. He hoped it was only rain, but he had seen snow in late September before. He broke into a slow trot. When he got to the hill overlooking Beth's house, he saw her waiting. She raised her hand and he waved back.

"I thought you weren't coming, but I'm happy to see you," she said.

"I wasn't sure if I could make it today, but Ma said you might be waiting for me, and Da said I mustn't keep a lady waiting. Thanks for waiting. I'm happy to see you too," JW said and felt himself blush again.

"Anything new?" Beth asked.

"Nothing new. Oh, yes there is. I took Tennyson home this morning."

"What did people say when they saw you with a rat?" Beth asked.

"No one knows," JW said and noticed the bewildered expression on Beth's face. "I took him out in my satchel," he said and tapped the leather case.

Beth moved away and asked, "Is he in there now?"

"No. I let him go in the barn. He turned back to look at me when I let him go. I'm not sure if he was saying thanks or was angry that I took him from his home."

"I thought you said he was getting better. Why did you take him home?"

JW explained to Beth that he had the night off and that Patty would be working his trap. "I was afraid he'd hit him with his shovel."

"I'm glad you took him out. Do you really think Patty would kill him?"

"Yes. Many of the men would do the same thing, but some see the rats, like the canaries, as a warning sign of a gas build-up. If they're leaving the mine, so are the men. Still, rats have been feared since the Middle Ages. Remember where the plague came from?"

"The fleas that infested the rats. Yes, I remember. But that's last year's history, and we've got to learn this year's," Beth said.

"Yes, I know. I'm going to try to stay for the day, but I'm pretty tired. I told Ma I'm going to sleep for the rest of the day and all night too," JW said and tried to stifle a big yawn.

The school came into view, and they hurried to get inside before the bell rang.

JW was surprised when at the end of first class Mr. Cantwell asked him some questions about the coal mine. He was more surprised when he was asked to go to the front of the class and tell his classmates what happens underground. He pulled the pictures from his satchel and told everyone that his father had drawn them. His classmates asked many questions. One of the new boys seemed particularly interested and JW spent his recess telling Davey Brown details his father had told him.

"You're not thinking about working in the pit, are you?" JW asked. "It's not where I'd be if I didn't have to."

"No, but I probably will end up involved in the coal mines, nonetheless," Davey said. "My father is the mine manager."

JW looked at Davey, but before he could respond, the bell rang, and they rushed back inside. Before long, JW knew he was done for the day. He packed up his satchel and quietly left the room. He didn't see the looks from Mr. Cantwell and Davey Brown, but he did see Beth smile, and he smiled back just as he pulled the door closed.

Chapter 35

"Hi, Ma," JW said as he entered the house. "I got the morning in. Well, most of it anyway." He started to tell her about school, but the thought of his bed won out, and he told her he would see her tomorrow morning. He climbed the stairs, and after placing the satchel on his dresser, he crawled under the blankets and was asleep almost immediately. Hours later, he woke up and looked out at the moon. Sleep overtook him again and, if he dreamed, he couldn't remember any of it in the morning.

Although it was early, he wasn't surprised to see his parents at the kitchen table having a cup of tea. He hurried outside to the toilet and then washed up in the small basin. After combing his hair, JW walked into the kitchen.

"Morning, JW. You'll be on time for school today," his father said. "It's only six o'clock."

"Morning, Da. I have to do some homework before I go. Morning, Ma. Can I study in the dining room?"

"Sure, dear. Go right in and I'll bring in a bite of breakfast for you. Do you want some eggs?" his mother asked. "Beth was here last night and left some papers for you. I put them on the table."

"Thanks, Ma. I'd rather porridge, if that's okay," JW said settling at the dining room table. He went over what he'd done the day before and read the homework he'd been given. Next, he went over the notes that Beth had left for him. The math was getting increasingly difficult. He'd have to stay for that class today; he was afraid he wouldn't be able to keep up otherwise.

He heard the clock's chimes announce it was eight o'clock and put his books and scribblers in the satchel, along with the lunch his mother had prepared for him, and hurried outside. Gulliver was there to greet him and walked with him to the hill overlooking Beth's house.

"Run on home, boy. I'll see you after school," JW said, petting him. He watched for a moment as Gulliver bounded toward home. Turning, he saw Beth come out of her house and he ran down to meet her. As they walked along, he felt Beth's hand slip into his. He turned to look at her and realized that this was the time to kiss her again. Afterwards, they laughed and ran hand in hand to school.

If JW had ever had a better day, he couldn't remember it. He stayed for every class and walked home with Beth.

He ate supper with his parents and heeded their words about going upstairs to get some sleep before his shift. Try as he might, he couldn't fall asleep. All he could think about was Beth. Finally, he fell asleep, but it seemed like only minutes before his mother's voice carried from the bottom of the stairs.

"Be right down, Ma," he called. The moon was full in the sky, and he gazed at it through his bedroom window as he drifted back to sleep.

"Hurry now. I thought you were up. It's past ten. You'll have to run part of the way," his mother said.

"Sorry, Ma. I fell asleep looking at the moon." He dressed quickly and was on his way in minutes.

—

Arriving at the mine, he saw Patty standing off on his own.

"Hi, Patty. How was your first night?"

"Hi, JW. The door stuck a few times, and Mickey's pa hollered at me, but Red was on the other side of the trap and told him to go easy on me. He don't seem so tough when he's talking to other full-grown men."

"He did the same thing to me, and the door wasn't even stuck," JW said. "Don't let it bother you."

"It's not as easy as I thought it'd be. I wish I hadda stayed at the breakers. I wonder if Red'd let me go back."

"He might," JW said, "but is that what you really want? The money's better at the trap, and once you get used to it, the only hard part is staying awake."

"I didn't sleep last night. I kept an eye out for the ghosts and rats. I jumped at every noise."

"Yeah, it can be spooky down there. What I do is think about my most favourite place I want to be and then pretend I'm off on some adventure."

"Whaddaya mean?" Patty asked.

"What do you like to do?"

"Fish, but playing baseball's my favourite," Patty said.

"Well then, think about the best game you ever played and close your eyes and try to remember everyone who was there that day. Who struck out? Who hit the home runs? And who won?" JW watched as Patty closed his eyes. After a few seconds, he saw a smile come over Patty's face and couldn't help smiling himself.

Patty opened his eyes, and his smile remained. "Holy gee, JW. I could see the field and even feel the sun on my face. I hit three homers that day."

"It'll work for your fishing trips too," JW said. As much as he felt the pit was the wrong place for him, he figured working underground was better for Patty than at the breakers.

He watched the rake start to fill up, and he and Patty made their way over and sat together. He missed Mickey and was glad that Patty was there.

"I'm getting used to the rake. How about you?" JW asked. It seemed that it was always travelling faster than it should.

"I'm getting used to it. I sat with Mickey last night, and he hollered all the way down, so no one could've heard me if I hadda made any noise," Patty said.

When the rake started its descent, JW hollered as loud as he could for as long as he could. Patty laughed beside him.

Chapter 36

The night passed slowly, and sleep beckoned him constantly, but JW knew better than to let Red catch him sleeping again. He threw the handful of oats that was left in the bottom of his satchel to the rats. They rushed forward, pushing and squealing, climbing over each other in their attempt to get to the oats first. JW noticed they stayed together in a pack but did not appear willing to share. The oats lasted less than a minute, and the rats looked his way hoping for more. They had to wait until he ate his lunch for the blackened crusts of bread with the tasty strawberry jam.

JW didn't see Mr. McGuire coming, but he heard him in plenty of time to have the door opening just as he came into view. There was a look of disappointment on Mickey's father's face when he made his way through. No words were exchanged. By shift's end, JW realized there was no way he could attend school that day. Staying for the entire day yesterday and not getting enough sleep meant he had to miss the whole day. Now he would really be behind. He heard Patty whistling as he came down the tracks. JW waited and walked with him to the rake.

"I'm so tired I don't even feel like washing up," JW said.

"I feel the same way," Patty said. "I'm going home and gonna sleep all day. I don't work until tomorrow or the next day. I better check with Red to be sure," he said, and JW watched as he ran over to Red once they reached the surface.

The water washed away the dirt and some of the weariness. JW was hopeful as he began the walk home, but by the time he passed the graveyard, he knew he wouldn't be heading to school. He took a slight detour and passed by Beth's house. He was glad to see she was outside. He was almost standing next to her when she turned from the clothesline.

"Oh, you startled me, JW," she said, her voice filled with surprise.

"Sorry. I just wanted to let you know I won't be going to school today. I'm just too tired."

"I'll bring over your homework, and I'll let Mr. Cantwell know that you won't be there. Should I tell him you'll be there tomorrow?" Beth asked. Her eyes searched JW's face.

"I hope so, so yes, please tell him I plan to be there tomorrow. But to be honest, if I don't start getting more sleep, it won't matter, because I didn't get last night's homework done, and now I'm going to miss today and then be two days behind." The frustration he was feeling was present in his voice, but JW kept his emotions in check. He turned to leave, walked a few steps then turned back to Beth. "Thanks for all your help. I'd never have been able to keep going without you."

Beth smiled. "Well, I don't want any excuses if I win any prizes this year."

"Oh, I'm pretty sure I won't be any competition for you. At least not this year. I'll see you tomorrow."

"See you then."

He slowed his pace as he started up the hill. He turned when he reached the top and was surprised Beth was still outside. He waved to her and waited until she waved back before heading toward home. Gulliver barked as JW neared the house. His tail wagged furiously in reaction to being petted. JW pushed his satchel around his back and stooped to pick up some logs for the fire. He heard Lightning whinny and dropped the logs. He decided he would clean out the stall first. The barn door swung open with a low groan. The hinges needed a little grease. He pulled the door shut behind him and laid his satchel on the floor.

He shovelled the manure from the stall, threw in some fresh hay and picked up some oats for Lightning to eat from his hand. "Hello, boy, how was your night? It's starting to get colder and I can see you're getting your winter coat. You're going to need that when we haul the wood home." JW brushed some loose hair from Lightning's back. "See you later, boy." He was surprised and happy to see Tennyson standing by the satchel, sniffing it, looking for oats. Scooping some up, he called out, "Hey, Tennyson, I thought you'd have found a whole lot of food by now. Here you go, boy." JW dropped the oats onto the floor, and Tennyson scurried over by his feet. He stood and watched the rat eat his fill. Tennyson soon disappeared through a passageway in the hay.

Chapter 37

"Breakfast is ready," Mary Donaldson said to her son as she heard the back door close behind him.

"Today it's supper, Ma. I'm too tired to think of anything but sleep. I stopped by Beth's and told her I wouldn't be going today. It's only October and I've already missed a week of school, not counting the half days. That's more than I missed in the first nine years. I really want to keep going, but I don't know how I can. I'm so tired all the time."

"Well, see how you feel tomorrow. The teachers said they understand," his mother said.

"I know, but I'm starting to fall behind. I'm missing too many math classes, and it's getting harder to catch up. But yes, I'll go to bed now and see what tomorrow brings."

JW trudged up the stairs, sad that he had to miss the day of school and sad that he wouldn't get to spend time with Beth. He hadn't wanted to tell his mother that he felt like giving up on school completely. She tried so hard and felt so bad that he couldn't attend like all the other children. But JW believed that the time was coming soon when he would just have to give up on his dream of finishing school. He knew he didn't need to finish to work in the mines, and he had enough education that he could one day be an overman like Red. The thought of walking all those tunnels for the next fifty years brought an involuntary shudder.

JW picked up *The Count of Monte Cristo* and tried to read a few lines, but sleep came quickly. He heard the book hit the floor just as his eyes closed. There were no dreams, good or bad, but he woke once to the sound of his parents' voices. His eyes closed, and he returned to the land of sleep and didn't wake again until he heard the clock strike eight. He had slept for twelve hours and felt rested.

Pulling on his clothes, he hurried down the stairs. JW saw that his mother was reading her prayer book, so he went to the kitchen and spread jam on some of the fresh-baked biscuits. The teapot was bubbling on the back of the stove. JW poured a cup and took the biscuits and tea into the dining room. He saw that Beth had been there with his homework. He started into the French lesson and felt comfortable with it after saying it aloud several times. He reached for his math book and saw a note sticking out of the pages. In her neat handwriting, Beth had informed him there was a math test the following day. Panic seized him as he looked at the notes that Beth had provided him. If he had known, he would have gotten up hours earlier. There was no way he could even get his homework done and it was absolutely impossible for him to review all the lessons he had done, as well as the ones he had missed. He only had an hour and a half before he had to leave for the pit. There was English and science homework as well. He started opening and closing books, slapping one closed before opening another.

"Is everything alright, dear?" his mother asked from the doorway.

"No, Ma, it isn't! I just found out I have a test tomorrow in math. I have a whole lot of other homework to do, so I don't know what to do first. And I only have a little over an hour before I have to head to work."

He watched as his mother pondered his dilemma. Her brow furrowed, and after a brief moment, she said, "Just do the most important work tonight, which I'm sure is the math. Let the other stuff go until you get more time."

The solution was so obvious, but JW hadn't been able to see it. "Thanks, Ma, that makes perfect sense. I can't get it all done, so I'll do what I can." He watched her smile as she walked toward the kitchen. He heard the oven door open, and the inviting smell of bread wafted into the dining room. A short time later, she brought him a piece of bread, dripping with butter and molasses. He ate holding the bread with his left hand while he scanned the math notes and tried the various equations. The clock chimed ten. JW did a few more equations before closing the books for the night. He packed the books into his satchel, careful not to wrinkle the pictures his father had drawn. His plan was to go directly to school from the coal mine.

"Ma, would you pack another sandwich? I'm going to go right to school after my shift."

"Sure thing. That's the spirit," Mary Donaldson said as she hugged him to her. She watched as he headed down the pathway toward the pit. She wished his cross were easier to bear, but at least he had a plan for tomorrow. *Tomorrow is promised to no man*, she recalled from her earlier reading. *Not promised to boys either*, she thought, and shivered.

Chapter 38

The weeks spent underground had made JW quite adept at hearing the trams long before they came into sight. He never planned on sleeping. It was just that sometimes when he blinked, his eyes took their time reopening, several minutes in some cases. Since getting caught by Red, JW had been careful to remain vigilant at all times. Tonight he believed would be no problem, because he had slept for half a day. As he rested with his back against the wall, he thought about the summer spent with Beth at the swimming hole and wished he had that to look forward to next year.

"Caught you, didn't I? Sleeping on the job. Are you trying to get everyone killed? Won't be so smart when I tell Red 'bout what I seen!" Shawn McGuire shouted at the top of his lungs.

JW came fully awake and slid down the wall to the floor of the tunnel. He rose to his feet and stared into the eyes of Mr. McGuire. "So, you're saying that you're going to squeal to the boss on me. I wonder what the other men will have to say about that when I tell them? Boy, won't Mickey be proud of you?"

JW watched as Shawn McGuire raised the shovel from the tram and started forward. "Da's a peaceful man, but if you hit me, you won't have anywhere you can hide. When I tell him what you plan to do, I'm sure he'll have something to say to you, Mr. McGuire." He watched as doubt crept into Shawn McGuire's eyes. He remembered what Patty had said about Mr. McGuire not being so tough when facing grown men, and the prospect of facing Andrew Donaldson seemed to make him rethink his plans to tell Red.

"I won't say anything this time, boy, but don't let me catch you again. Get the trap open, I ain't got all night."

JW watched as Shawn McGuire went through the trap door for what he hoped would be the last time this shift. He hoped, also, that he wouldn't tell Red, but he was more afraid that he might tell his father. His father would be angry that he had fallen asleep, but he would be furious that he'd been brazen enough to talk to his elders in such a manner. JW's eyes never closed for more than a second the rest of the shift. He was wide awake when Red greeted him in the morning.

"How was your night, JW? Tired?"

"No, sir. I slept half the day yesterday. I plan on staying the whole day at school today," JW said.

"Sorry to tell you, but Patty's grandpa died and he won't be in this morning, so you gotta stay till about noontime. Maybe you can get to school for the afternoon part."

"But I've got a math test this morning that I can't miss. I mean, I'm sorry about Patty's grandfather, but—"

"Someone's got to open the trap, and you're it. If I had someone else, I wouldn't make you miss your test, but you can't leave until someone comes to relieve you. See you."

JW felt dejected as he watched Red walk toward the travelling way. After all his studying he was going to miss the test. He wasn't even tired, but he couldn't go to school. He threw his satchel on the ground and went over to the trap door. There was nothing he could do. He pulled the door open as Smitty came to a halt.

"I thought you had school?"

"I do, but Patty can't come in today because his grandfather died." When he said the words, he realized how selfish he sounded. Poor Patty, losing his grandfather. "I was supposed to have a math test today, but I'm here until someone comes to replace me. I'm pretty much sure that I won't be able to keep going anyway, and missing this test means that I'll be too far behind to keep going, especially if I can only go a couple of days a week. At least Tennyson got out," he said.

"What?"

"I took him out and set him free. Looks like it's just me stuck down here."

"I'm sorry to hear that, but maybe it'll all work out. Hey, Tennyson got out," Smitty said, and clucked his tongue to move the horse along.

JW walked over to his satchel and picked it up. He brushed off the leather, happy to see he hadn't damaged it. He remembered how much work his grandfather had put into making it for him. He had loved his grandfather and felt ashamed of his comments when he considered how badly Patty must be feeling.

"What are you doing here? I thought you had a big test today."

JW turned to the voice of his father. "I did, but Patty's grandpa died and I have to cover the trap. It's getting too hard to do anyway. I may as well face the fact that I'm all done with school. Maybe I'll get you to show me how to swing the pick. Pulling down those ceilings will have to be my adventures. I don't want to stay on the trap door for too long. There is only so much of Shawn McGuire a man can take."

"I've got to get on up ahead, but we'll talk later," Andrew Donaldson said, patting his son's shoulder. He glanced back at JW just as the trap door closed and saw the slumped shoulders. *Only so much of Shawn McGuire a man can take.* Wasn't that the truth. In a short number of weeks, JW had gone from being a carefree boy to seeing himself as a man. What had he been thinking? Sure, the trap door was relatively safe, but he would have to move on from there. The thought of his only child swinging a pick into the ceiling to release tons of coal to the floor below sent a series of shivers up and down his spine. But he knew JW would not be content to pull a trap door all day long. He would have to train him well. Pictures wouldn't work this time.

Chapter 39

Beth looked up the hill hoping to see JW. She didn't know his plan had been to go to school directly from work. She would have to leave in another minute. As the seconds sped by, she kept her eyes focused on the top of the hill overlooking her house. Saddened, she started on her trek to school. She walked slowly, as she held out hope that he was simply running late and could still make it. Once she saw the school come into view, she knew he would not attend today. She also knew that it was unlikely he would be back this year. Beth looked over her shoulder one last time as she climbed the steps to the school. Mr. Cantwell glanced past her when she entered the room – he too hoped John Wallace would be there. Beth shook her head and took her seat. The bell rang to signal the start of the first class and the start of the all-important math test.

Chapter 40

By noontime, JW was feeling tired, so he was glad to see Red coming toward him with a boy following closely behind. The introductions were made and JW started on his way to the surface. He heard Red call out.

"Are you on your way to school then?"

"No, it's too late. I think I'm all done with that now. See you later." He was too tired to care and just wanted to wash up and go home and sleep until it was time to go to work again. With his father working today, he would have to remember to get in some coal and wood before going to bed.

There was a chill in the air as he trudged along the road. He didn't lift his eyes to marvel at the clouds filled to bursting with rain or possibly snow. He kicked a few pebbles as he walked and didn't hear Gulliver until he was beside him. "Hiya, boy. Always good to see you." Gulliver's nose tapped JW's hand the rest of the way home; he wanted his master to pet him. JW stopped and knelt down beside his friend and hugged him, petting his shoulders and head. All was right with the world for Gulliver. JW's satchel banged heavily against his thigh. It was filled with school books, pictures and things he had picked up here and there. He would empty most of its contents today. He still wanted to use it to carry his lunch.

Lightning moved aside as JW cleaned out his stall, and he stood still while being brushed. The horse's winter coat, getting thicker, gleamed with each stroke of the brush. There was no sign of Tennyson this morning. Perhaps he had found a mate, or at least some place warm to sleep away his days. The wind had picked up, and JW was glad he and his father had done some repairs to the barn the past summer. At least Lightning and Tennyson would be warm this winter. JW dropped some oats on the floor in case Tennyson was having difficulty finding food. He pitched some hay for Lightning, petted him and headed toward the woodpile. He heard the back door open and saw his mother standing there.

"Your father already brought in the coal and wood I'll be needing for the day. Why aren't you in school?"

JW told her about Patty's grandpa, and she said she was sorry to hear about old Amos but said that he'd had a good, long life and that he had seemed old even when she had been a girl.

"I'm so sorry you missed today, but tomorrow's another day. Try again then."

"You know, Ma, I think I'll just concentrate on getting sleep and doing my job. It's not working out trying to do both."

"But you've been doing grand so far. Beth's been bringing the lessons you need and helping with the notes and all."

"I know, Ma, and you and Da have been helping me too. I can't keep expecting Beth to bring my homework every other day. Soon, there'll be a foot or two of snow down, and she can't make that walk all the time. No, I think it's best if I just get used to the idea of work. Besides," he said in a more upbeat voice, "I already asked Da to teach me how to swing a pick, so I can move off the trap door. Don't want to be a trapper boy all my life," he said, forcing a laugh and sitting down at the kitchen table. He was hungry and ate a good meal, washing the eggs down with some hot tea.

"Thanks, Ma, that was great. If I'm not up by nine-thirty you better wake me." As he started up the stairs, he turned to his mother. "Please tell Beth thanks for everything, but that I won't be going to school anymore. I don't want her wasting her time bringing the lessons. Tell her I'll see her on my next day off. Goodnight, Ma."

—

Mary Donaldson watched as John Wallace walked up the stairs then sat at the kitchen table with a cup of tea in front of her. Prayers and thoughts of what could be done to help her son ran through her mind. The tea turned cold and she poured it out. The stew wouldn't cook itself, so she began the preparation for the evening meal.

Chapter 41

"Hi, Beth."

Beth turned to see who had spoken. Davey Brown stood close to the door. "Oh hi, Davey," Beth said.

"I thought JW was coming today."

"I thought so too, but I guess he was just too tired after working all night. I know he was planning on being here."

"Perhaps he should have taken the night off. This was an important test," Davey said.

"He's not working there because he wants to!" Beth said defensively.

"The shifts have been cut by the mine owners, so it takes both John Wallace and his father working to barely scrape by. He wanted to go to college and travel the world. I never thought he'd have to go underground." Tears welled up, and Beth turned her head and blinked them away. She picked up her books and walked from the room and down the stairs.

Davey watched her go, sad that he had upset her and wishing there was something he could do to help.

Chapter 42

Andrew swung the pick with more force than needed, and a large piece of the roof came free. He stepped out of the way quickly. His adrenaline was pumping. He just wanted the shift to be over so he could get home. He thought maybe he could work JW's shifts for him, but they were quite often the same as his own, and any others would mean working a double. That wasn't the answer. He swung again and grunted as the pick buried itself in the coal. He pulled and twisted it free, then swung again and more coal fell to the floor.

"Swinging a little hard, aren't you, Andy?" Red said from behind him.

"I s'pose I might be, a little," Andrew said.

"Something bothering you?"

"Yeah. JW should be in school and not down here with the likes of Shawn McGuire, or me for that matter. With the way the work is being cut back, soon Mary will have to find a job too."

"I can't say I'm gonna miss this place. Well, maybe a little, but I've worked as much as I've wanted since becoming shift boss. I don't know how you're making do on the few shifts coming your way," Red said.

"That's why my boy's down here."

"I gotta few weeks left, then it's off to do some fishing. I don't plan on missing too many sun-ups or sundowns. I'm gonna sleep nights and enjoy the days."

"I hope you do just that. You deserve a good retirement. You'll surely be missed. God help us with who'll replace you," Andrew said.

"I was wanting to ask your thoughts on that very thing. Soon as you pull a bit more from the ceiling, let's have a talk."

Andrew swung the pick and watched the last of the ceiling break free. He put down his pick, and walked to where Red stood waiting.

Chapter 43

JW fell into the rhythm of working and sleeping. Before long, Patty returned to work. He told JW that he had been a little nervous standing next to the body of his granddad and that his cousin had told him he'd seen his hand move. But that then he'd remembered that his granddad had always taken him fishing and for walks in the woods, and after that he was no longer afraid. JW was a little nervous himself that night and spent much of it looking behind him and peering into the shadows, hoping Patty's granddad didn't make an appearance.

He hadn't spoken to Beth since deciding to give up on school, but he'd seen her from a distance, walking with Davey Brown. He hoped he and Beth could still be friends even though he was not in school, but he realized that their paths would be very different from now on. The thought saddened him. The satchel at his side was much lighter these days, now that he was no longer carrying school books in it. He used it mostly to carry his lunch. He had decided to leave the pictures of the mine in the satchel, the ones that his father had drawn. He wanted to keep them close by so that he could familiarize himself with the workings of the mine. If he was going to be stuck down there, he wanted to know as much as his father did.

JW knew that it would take time to learn all he wanted to know, but in the short time he'd been there he managed to get used to the trap door, and the rats no longer scared him. He hoped he could move to shovelling coal soon, but for now he was content to work the trap. He lit his headlamp and pulled the pictures from the satchel. They truly did lay out the mine very well. He heard the sound of sleigh bells and was pleased to see Smitty round the turn. He shoved the pictures back in his satchel and walked to the door.

"Sorry to hear you had to leave school, son," Smitty said.

"Thanks," JW said. "I would have liked to have been able to stay, but there was no way I could. Maybe I'll try again next year."

"Sure, that might work," Smitty said, though they both knew that was unlikely. The pause that followed stretched to almost a minute before JW spoke.

"But, I'm going to make the most of this year and try to learn everything about working down here."

"That's the best thing to do then. Remember to keep reading, and if you already have the school books, keep reading those, so you'll be ready for next year. You'll do fine down here. Just be sure to keep your eyes open." Lowering his voice, Smitty added, "There's more like Shawn McGuire that work underground, so be on your guard, and keep your eyes open." He pulled up on the reins, and JW opened the trap door to let him through.

He watched for a moment as Smitty and the horse went out of sight before closing the door. He thought about Smitty's advice, or was it perhaps a warning? He would be sure to keep his eyes open, both on his job as a trapper boy and to watch out for the not-so-nice characters. He remembered Red had told him much the same thing: *Not all the fellas you meet down here are friendly-like.*

He heard the men coming and was glad the shift was over. He waved to his father, who was working the day shift. Washing up and the walk home were tedious but all part of his job. He saw Gulliver coming from a long way off, and the dog stayed by his side as he cleaned Lightning's stall and cut some kindling. JW returned to the barn with some split logs. He had decided to pile some of them inside to keep them dry, as there was lots of room in the barn. He saw Tennyson move out from behind the logs. His limp was barely noticeable. It would never be gone, but it was much better. Before JW realized what was happening, Tennyson bristled and Gulliver lunged for him.

"No, Gulliver! Don't!" Gulliver stopped, but Tennyson kept coming, and JW had to scoop him from the floor before Gulliver hurt or killed him.

"Hold on, you two. You'll have to learn to live together." JW held Tennyson and let Gulliver sniff him to get his scent. Tennyson pushed against JW's hand, trying to get away. After a few moments the rat calmed down, and JW laid him on the floor, where the rat ate some oats before scurrying back to his home behind the woodpile. Gulliver looked anxiously toward the spot where Tennyson had gone, but JW knelt beside the dog and petted his head as he asked him to be nice to Tennyson. JW left the barn, hoping for the best. His mother was hanging out the wash, her hands red from the cold October wind. She was humming a tune as she pulled the bedclothes from the pail.

"I'll get you a bite to eat in a moment, dear."

"I'll fix myself some porridge, Ma. Want a hand with the clothes?"

"Thanks just the same, dear, but I can manage. If you wait a few minutes, I'll fix you a proper breakfast too."

"I'm not going to school, so I can make my own. Besides, I like porridge. I think it helps me sleep better."

"If you don't mind then, that'll be a help," his mother said and smiled.

With the porridge eaten and the dishes in the sink, JW went to his room. He pulled the pictures from the satchel and laid them out on the floor. He blew the dust off, and when he assembled them in the proper order they showed the entire working of the mine. Having spent the past month and a half underground, JW better understood what the pictures represented and how each job was interconnected. He thought about the men pulling the coal from the earth and how it was transported along tracks, through the trap door, to the surface. The young breaker boys waited to pull the rocks and shale from the coal. Many of them, like Patty, waited for an opportunity to work below as a trapper boy, and if they were lucky and their hands intact, they might go on to be full-fledged miners some day. For some it would happen, but for others, perhaps with injured hands, it was only a dream. It was a nightmare for JW – and it seemed that it would be a recurring one for years to come.

His hands traced over the pictures and he took a moment to appreciate the talent his father possessed. He had never known before that his father could draw so well and that it had been JW's grandfather who had taught him.

JW hadn't realized that the iron and leather products, made by his grandfather, were sketched prior to being completed. He also learned that his father had considered becoming a blacksmith, like his own father. Perhaps there was a lot more he didn't know about his father and mother. He wondered what their dreams had been.

Working in the mines would kill dreams in a hurry. There was little time to dream when you always had to have your eyes open. He figured his mother's dreams were tempered by the lack of money coming into the household. JW put the pictures back in his satchel, and got ready for bed. As soon as he lay down, he felt the comforting arms of sleep envelope him, and he slept soundly until the sound of his mother's footsteps rushed up the stairs.

"John Wallace! Get up, dear! There's been a cave-in at the mine. You have to go help. Hurry along. There's men trapped."

JW pulled his clothes on, rushed down the stairs and was on his way out the door when his mother called to him.

"Take this with you," she said, handing him his satchel. "It's your lunch. You could be there all night. Please be careful." She hugged him and kissed his cheek before he headed out the door and on his way to the mine. He noticed the prayer book in her hands.

JW could hear the commotion as he arrived at the wash house. Red was there barking orders, trying to keep the men organized. A mine rescue crew headed down the travelling way, as a few men came up to report the damage. JW stood by, listening as one of the men spoke. "There's six men trapped. Smitty, Shawn McGuire, his son Mickey, two new fellas, and Andy. It's mostly Tunnel Seven. The roof let go and a couple of the timbers cracked. There must be close to a hundred ton of coal in the tunnel! What little air there is in there won't last long."

Red noticed JW standing behind him. "We can't be sure. There could be an air pocket in there to last a while." The man who had spoken first saw JW and quickly agreed with Red.

"Sure, probably could be some air in there."

JW knew they were trying not to alarm him, but he also knew that he had to get below to try to help his father and the other men. He grabbed a pick and shovel and headed down the tunnel. He heard Red call to him, but he ignored him. He had to try to help his father. Patty was at the trap door when JW arrived.

"Sorry 'bout your pa," Patty said.

"What do you mean?"

"Him and the rest all trapped in the tunnel with no way out. Sorry."

"Open the door, Patty. I gotta go and help get them out." JW rushed along the track and saw several men shovelling coal from the face of the tunnel. He realized the man hadn't exaggerated the amount of coal. There could be a hundred ton filling the tunnel. There was only a narrow passageway for the men to work in their rescue effort, and all were able to swing a pick and use a shovel better than he. He knew he would only slow them down.

JW stood for a moment, praying, watching the men, trying to stay out of their way. He felt he had to do something and scraped some of the coal away. The speed of the pan shovels increased as the men raced against time to free their friends. Suddenly, they stopped shovelling, and one man brushed away some coal. Then JW heard the tinkling of bells and saw the head of Smitty's horse as the miner uncovered it. The looks exchanged between the two shovellers sent a wave of fear through JW. He guessed it would take close to half an hour to uncover the body of the horse. Then they still had to move it out of their way in order to resume their rescue attempt.

JW watched for another minute or so, then hurried deeper into the mine, away from the tunnel where his father and others were trapped, perhaps hurt or dying. He tried to push the thought from his mind as he carried the pick and dragged the shovel along behind him, metal on metal as it clanged against the rail. His satchel tapped against his leg. He slowed as he neared the tunnel where he and Mickey had gone on their treasure hunt. It was all worked out and abandoned, but he knew it was close to the other end of Tunnel Seven. He believed that only three or four feet separated the tunnels. His mind raced as he wondered what to do next.

JW pulled the pictures from his satchel, and turned up the flame on his headlamp. He scanned them briefly then put them away and grabbed the pick. He looked to his left, then to his right, searching the wall for a place to begin. Hoping he'd made the right choice, he swung the pick with all his might. He hadn't used a pick much, and it stuck deep into the wall. Working it up and down, he managed to wrench it free. The next swing, he used a little less force, and a piece of the wall broke away. He continued to swing at an angle, and bigger pieces gave way.

JW's first concern was to try to break a hole through to provide air into the tunnel. He had to chip away a huge piece of the wall in order to be able to dig deeper. He dug closer to the floor so that the roof would hold. The last thing he wanted was to cause another cave-in. He guessed that he was about two feet deep in his digging when he thought he heard a tapping sound coming from behind the wall. Adrenaline surging through his body caused him to swing the pick too hard, and it lodged deep into the wall. Pulling the pick out, he swung again, and this time saw a large portion break free. He listened again and knew he could hear tapping, as he heard the sound from the other side grow louder.

Suddenly, some coal fell toward him, and JW realized that someone was digging from the other side. A pick head came through the opening. He stepped back in surprise, as Shawn McGuire scurried through the small hole, followed by the two new men, who appeared shaken. "Thank you, thank you," they both said. Mickey was next through and then Smitty. JW held his breath until he finally saw his father emerge from the tunnel. He hugged his father, almost lifting him off the ground.

"So it was you that figured how to get us out," his father said. "How?"

"Mickey and I went exploring one night, and when we came to this point I could hear sound coming through the wall. I spent this morning looking at the pictures you drew, and I remembered where the tunnels almost converge."

Excitement filled the air as Smitty and Mickey came over, clapping him on the shoulders, thanking him. Finally Shawn McGuire said, "Thanks, boy. You done real good." This was high praise from Mickey's father, who had been nothing but misearable to JW before now.

Bobbing lights came toward them as Red, Mr. Brown, the mine manager, and another man in a suit and tie arrived. There were looks of relief on their faces as Red

counted the six men who had been trapped. "Thank God," Red said. Mickey piped up, "Yes, Red, and you can thank JW too. He's the one got us out. Him and his pa."

Red smiled at JW. "Way to go, boy." Red hurried the men from the area. He wanted to get them checked over and get the story from them.

JW squeezed his father's hand as he left with Red. "I'll see you on the surface, Da. I think you need to wash up." Everyone seemed to be walking well and there didn't seem to be any blood. JW listened as Mr. Brown spoke to the other man. The two of them were not dressed to be underground, and seemed uncomfortable in the dust and darkness. He listened as Mr. Brown spoke of Red's retiring and of how difficult it was going to be to replace him.

"There's no one that can fill his spot. No one who knows the workings of all the different jobs," Mr. Brown said.

"Excuse me, sir," JW said, interrupting the manager.

"Yes, what is it, lad?"

"My father knows every job that takes place underground and above as well."

"What does he do?" Mr. Brown asked.

"He's a pick miner, sir, but he knows all the other jobs too," JW said.

"It's nice to see a lad proud of his dad, but I need someone who knows every facet of every job. Good day to you. You did a wonderful thing here today getting the men out," Mr. Brown said and began to leave.

JW picked up his satchel from beneath a pile of coal, and reached into it. Pulling the pictures out, he called after Mr. Brown. "Excuse me, sir, would you please take a look at these?"

With obvious impatience, Mr. Brown turned back. "What is it then?" Taking the pictures from JW's outstretched hand, he nodded as he glanced at each one. "Did you draw these, lad?"

"No, sir, my father did, and he explained how each job tied into the other." Taking the pictures back, JW laid them out in sequence, which showed how each job was interconnected. "My father, Andrew Donaldson, who was one of the trapped men and helped get them out, knows how the ventilation system works and all the underground jobs too. He even took me to the breakers to show me what happens to the coal once it's above ground. I think he could replace Red, sir," JW said.

"You do, do you? Well tell your father to come and see me tomorrow. Tell him Mr. Brown wants to speak with him. What's your name, lad?"

"John Wallace Donaldson, sir."

"Mind if I keep these pictures overnight? I'd like to have a closer look at them. I'll give them back to your father tomorrow."

"That would be fine, sir. Thank you, Mr. Brown," JW said and turned to leave. "Goodbye, sir."

"Goodbye, John Wallace."

Chapter 44

JW waited outside for his father. He saw him coming toward him. The ordeal of the cave-in could not be washed away with soap and water – it was still present in his eyes. His father smiled an uncertain smile as he came alongside JW. They started on their way home and moments later put arms around each other's shoulders like boyhood friends. Neither said a word, just breathing in the clean air. They both looked at the sky, marvelling at the broad array of colours on the trees below the magnificent blue. All thoughts of the coal mine left their minds. Before long, Gulliver came racing toward them. With JW and his father petting him, Gulliver bounded from one to the other, his wagging tail slapping against their pant legs.

Mary Donaldson held the door open for her two men. She smiled, relieved, as they crossed the threshold.

"There's a pot of stew ready. Can you eat?" she asked.

JW blushed a little as his father took his mother into his arms and kissed her for a long time. Her face was a little flushed when Andrew released her.

"He saved us. Me and five others are alive because of his actions."

JW sat and listened as his father heaped praise upon him. The stew was hot, and he realized he was quite hungry after the first spoonful. He watched as his father's food turned cold while he retold the story of how his son had been so smart and how he knew right where to dig to get them out. JW looked at the clock and knew he should get some more sleep before his upcoming shift.

"I've got to get some more sleep. Ten o'clock's not far away." He rose and headed to the stairs. "Goodnight, Ma, Da."

"Goodnight, son," they said together.

"Ma, my lunch is still good. I didn't eat any of it."

"I'll pack you a fresh lunch. Try and get some rest, dear. Goodnight."

Chapter 45

His father had been the one to wake him. More stew awaited him as he made his way down the stairs. After a quick wash, he managed to eat a good amount. As promised, his lunch was fresh. Strawberry jam sandwiches and a couple of molasses cookies. He was so glad that his father was okay, and he saw the appreciation in both his mother's and father's faces. He hugged them both as he left.

JW didn't mind the walk to the pit that evening. His fear of the dark wasn't completely gone, but unless he heard a spooky sound in the night, he was okay. Mind you, he didn't spend much time peering into the dark woods. Gulliver walked part of the way with him at night and that was enough.

There was a loud cheer as he entered the wash house. He wondered what was going on until several men approached him and lifted him on their shoulders. After what seemed like a long time, they set him down. He was clapped on the back and had his hair ruffled many times over before everything quieted down. The ever-present

Red was there. It was like he never slept. JW took his seat on the rake and lowered his head. He was surprised when, at the last moment, Shawn McGuire sat next to him. After a moment, Shawn cleared his throat.

"I just want to thank you for saving my boy. You're a smart one alright, just like Mickey says." Then they both bowed their heads as if in prayer and readied themselves for the descent.

That shift, and the next several days, seemed to fly by. Now, only the ones who had been in the cave-in acknowledged him with a clap on the back or, if it was Mickey, an arm around the neck. The accolades had been great, but JW was glad things were back to normal. He was relieved night shift was over, and he had a day off before starting on the day shift. He washed up and decided he would take his time before heading home. The walk to town was only a couple of miles, and he knew he had lots of time to sleep later. It would be a good time to pick up a few supplies at the Co-op.

The bell above clanged as JW pulled the door open. It clanged again as he closed it. He saw the man behind the counter look up and smile.

"Hello, Mr. Ferneyhough," JW said.

"Why hello, John Wallace. What brings you in today?"

"I need a new pair of gloves, and I was going to pick up a few candies," JW said as he reached into the bin with the gloves and pulled out a pair. His eyes fell to the scribblers on a nearby shelf, then he looked away. He placed the gloves on the counter and asked for two cents worth of candy. He watched as Mr. Ferneyhough tallied the items.

"That'll be eighteen cents, John Wallace."

"Just mark it on my bill, sir."

"Can't do that, son," Mr. Ferneyhough said.

"Pardon?"

"Your father closed out your account yesterday."

JW frowned as he reached into his pocket and pulled nine cents out, half of what he needed. He looked at the gloves and candies on the counter, dropped two cents and picked up the candies. He placed the gloves back in the bin.

"Thank you, sir," JW said and heard the bell clanging as he pulled the door shut behind him.

—

The long walk home was filled with questions. *Why would Da close my account? I always pay it, and I don't waste money. Well, maybe a few candies. But it's my money.* The questions continued to run through his mind, and he didn't see or hear Gulliver coming. When Gulliver nudged his fingers, JW jumped, then laughed when he looked into the expectant face of his loyal, trusted friend.

"You scared me, boy – and it's daytime."

Gulliver's response was to raise his head and do his full-body shuffle.

"Thanks for coming to meet me, boy," JW said, and rubbed the dog's head. The rest of the fifteen-minute walk was in silence, other than the crunching of rocks underfoot.

JW's thoughts were jumbled, and he made a mental note to get back the pictures his father had drawn from Mr. Brown. In all the excitement of the cave-in, JW had forgotten to tell his father that Mr. Brown wanted to see him. He didn't know what he truly expected Mr. Brown to do, but he wanted him to know his father was a smart man. It had been almost a week since he'd given the mine manager the pictures.

A few of the chickens were scratching about in the yard, the younger ones mimicked the older ones in their search for food. He noticed the barn door was open and ran to close it. He didn't want to have to chase after Lightning, although he knew Lightning would come at the sight of some oats. JW was surprised to see his father brushing the horse's coat.

His father turned to him. "We have to haul some wood soon, so I thought I'd spruce him up a bit before I put the bridle and traces on him. You want to brush him some?"

"No, he seems to be enjoying what you're doing."

"I saw your rat. I think he's got a girlfriend."

JW felt the blood rush to his cheeks. "What?"

"Oh, I saw you let him outta your satchel. Bad leg and all, he seems to be getting around pretty good." Andrew Donaldson put down the brush. "Let's go have some breakfast."

JW held the kitchen door open for his father.

"How come you're so late?" his father asked as they took their places at the table.

JW thanked his mother as she placed eggs in front of him. Then he looked at his father. "I went to the Co-op today after my shift to pick up some supplies."

"Is that so? How is Mr. Ferneyhough?"

"He seemed well, but when I tried to buy my supplies, I mean, put them on my account, Mr. Ferneyhough told me my account had been closed ... by you." JW looked from his father to his mother, then back to his father. "Did I do something wrong? Am I being punished? I only bought some candies and a scribbler, other than gloves, last time."

"No, you didn't do anything wrong. It's just that only miners and people with jobs can have an account," his father said.

JW looked at his father. "I don't know...."

"Your father shut your account, because starting to-morrow you're back in school," Mary Donaldson said, smiling. "Full-time."

"What?"

"I have a new job. Red's job. Mr. Brown called me into his office, and we had a long talk. Apparently, somebody told him I knew quite a bit about the mine but failed to let me know that Mr. Brown wanted to speak to me," Andrew said, smiling. He pushed the pictures across the table.

"His son Davey told him that you had told the entire class about my drawings and about how the mine works. It means more money and full-time work, so you don't need a job anymore. Hopefully I can keep things running as smoothly as Red did and over time have better work-ing conditions for the men."

—

JW's excitement was such that he could hardly contain himself. He went outside and shovelled out Lightning's stall and gave him extra hay and a handful of oats. He saw Tennyson slip into the stall to share in the bounty. A moment later another rat joined him. JW suspected this was the girlfriend his father had mentioned earlier.

Leaving the barn, JW bent down and hugged Gulliver again. "I'm going back to school, full-time, boy. You'll be seeing lots more of me around here." The full-body shuffle said it all: Gulliver was happy too.

JW had been too excited to eat earlier but felt his stomach grumble and went back into the house. He bounded up the stairs and went to his bedroom. The money he had managed to save he took from the jar on his bedside table and put in his pocket. The unfinished novel, *The Count of Monte Cristo,* stood out on his bookshelf. He pulled it down and opened it to the last page he'd read, then laid it face down on his bed for later.

"Hope it ends well," he said to himself.

He went down the stairs as quickly as he'd gone up. The smell of fish cakes got his attention, and JW put two on his plate. The tea was hot and the biscuits warm.

"I would have got that for you," his mother said as she entered the kitchen. She held a pair of rabbits in her hands. "I was planning on making you another stew, but maybe a rabbit pie would be nice for a change."

"That would be great, Ma," JW said. "When can I start back to school?"

"Why, tomorrow, of course. Your mining days are over for now. Hope you never have to go back." His mother put her arms around him and hugged him for a long time.

JW pulled the money from his pocket and laid it on the table. "I was saving up to get you and Beth each something for Christmas, but it might come in handy for something else."

"You keep it, dear," his mother said. She reached into the cupboard and placed the silver dollar he'd won back on grading day on the table with the other money. "I couldn't bear to spend your hard-earned dollar. So you take your money and spend it on whatever you want."

—

JW took his time walking to town. As he was about to pass his grade eight teacher's house, he noticed she was in her yard. She looked up as he came near her fence.

"Oh hi, John Wallace. How are you? I was sorry to hear you had to leave school, but you have to be commended for trying so hard. Perhaps next year. Maybe things will pick up."

JW listened politely, waiting as she spoke, but he couldn't hold back his good news any longer. "Da took another job, and I start back to school full-time tomorrow."

Mrs. Johnson opened the gate and hugged him. "I am so happy for you. If you need any help, just ask."

JW thanked her and continued on his way. He walked up the few steps and knocked on the door of his friend

Mickey's house and came face to face with Shawn Mc-Guire.

"C'mon in, son. Mickey's at the table. I hear your pa took Red's job."

"Yes, sir, he did," JW said.

"Guess there'll be lots of changes then?"

"Da said he'd like to keep it running as smoothly as Red has it. He said with all the experienced men like you and the others, he should be able to."

"Why don't you have a cuppa tea with Mickey?" Shawn said.

JW took his shoes off by the door and joined Mickey at the table. Mickey's mother poured a cup of tea and put a biscuit and jam on the table for him.

"I hear your da took Red's job. Guess you'll get all the easy work now," Mickey said, then laughed.

JW looked at his friend. "With Da working full-time, I won't be working anymore. I start back to school tomorrow."

"I figured you might. Good for you, JW," Mickey said.

"Maybe we could still meet on some of your days off and—"

"Sure, sure. Ole Long Jack might let an above-ground-er travel for free."

They talked a little longer and tried hard to laugh and keep the conversation light, but as he closed the door behind him, JW felt like he was losing his best friend for the second time in his life.

Chapter 46

JW stood on the hill overlooking Beth's house. He watched as she came outside to start on her way to school. He smiled as she glanced to where he stood. She took a second look and realized that it was him. She dropped her books and ran to meet him halfway up the hill. She hugged him fiercely when she reached him, looking at the books in his arms.

"What? Are you coming to school today?"

"Today and the rest of the year. Da took Red's old job, and he'll get more shifts, so I don't have to work anymore. Except I'm going to have to spend the next month trying to catch up. I sure hope Mr. Cantwell will let me make up the tests I missed."

"Oh, I'm sure he will. He seemed really disappointed when I told him that you had to quit."

"That's good." JW paused. "Uh, I saw you walking with Davey Brown. Is he your boyfriend?" he asked, holding his breath while he waited for her answer.

"Well, he is kind of cute," Beth said. She looked at JW's crestfallen face and bent forward and kissed him. "But there's only one boy for me, JW."

JW felt Beth's hand slip into his and took a deep breath of the crisp November air.

The End

Acknowledgements

My sincere thanks to Cape Breton University Press.

I would also like to thank the following people for their assistance: Tom Miller (Director of the Glace Bay Miner's Museum), Wish Donovan (underground guide at the Miner's Museum), Jack Humphries, Shelley Johnson and Donald MacGillivray, who was always available to answer a question or two. Thanks to all the boys and men who toiled underground and the women who awaited their return.

Thank you to Kate Kennedy for all the editorial suggestions and for making such a positive impact on the novel. Most of all, thank you to Joanne for her love and support and for reading everything I write.

H.R.M.

Praise for Trapper Boy

From the blog of British writer Robert Southworth:

"Trapper Boy is a beautifully crafted story that takes place in a tiny town in Cape Breton, Nova Scotia, Canada. The setting could be any place in the world that relies principally upon the extraction industries for jobs (both natural gas/oil and coal). [...] Miners share a culture that unites them regardless of where they live – a true brotherhood.

In *Trapper Boy* I read about the agonizing choice the parents had to make in sending their son to the darkness of the mines and knew I wanted to purchase more copies to give to my grandchildren who take education and their quality of life for granted. My 14 year old grandson actually put away his electronic gadgets and read the book. He is using this novel in his English class.

This book will not bore the young readers as it's not filled with pages of dry historical information. I truly enjoyed the beautifully drawn well-placed sketches that help bring to life the hardships of underground life for the boys and men that toiled there. It has a wonderful plot that drew me and my grandson in and gave us common ground to share. Don't just purchase the book; read it and talk about it to your children, grandchildren and have them imagine what life once was for children their age."

http://robsbook.blogspot.co.uk/p/authors-continued.html

Charlottetown *Guardian* December 29, 2012.

"This is another very good book, especially for a 'first published novel'. Mr. MacDonald makes conditions and routine in the mine so vivid.... The language is plain, but correct. The illustrations by Michael MacDonald are rough but accurate in detail, (just how someone with a good eye and no training would draw)."

CM Magazine, Vol. XIX No 16, December 21, 2012

"MacDonald uses vivid, carefully selected, symbolic detail in presenting the underground world."

"Hugh R. MacDonald manages to educate without being didactic, and his upbeat ending has a bittersweet element which makes it realistic. Trapper Boy is excellent literature and ought to win prizes. Congratulations to the author and to Cape Breton University Press for bringing this novel into being."

"Highly Recommended."

About the author

Hugh R. MacDonald is an award-winning writer of fiction and enjoys the company of other writers. He has been fortunate to belong to a local writing group for years and attends workshops that include renowned Cape Breton and Canadian authors. Hugh has been a member of the Writers Federation of Nova Scotia for many years. His work has been published online and in two anthologies. Hugh is a graduate of Cape Breton University and works in the human service field. He resides in Cape Breton with his wife, Joanne. At the time of printing, he is busy on his next project, a mainstream novel set in Cape Breton. *Trapper Boy* is his first published novel.